<u>Now available on V</u>
<u>Packa</u>

Blame It On The Drako use code RB17020 if
ordering through Walkenhorst's

Acknowledgments
Bulletproof Love and Respect

Round 2... The saga continues. I want to take this opportunity to salute and thank my loyal supporters. Thank you. Without you the flame dies out and the vision is too dark to see. FREE ALL MY BROTHERS OF THE STRUGGLE!!! Thank you, God, for putting a solid one in the right position to win, even in a losing situation.

To every dreamer, visionary and entrepreneur, city 2 city — I see you. Let's run it up. Secure the bag!

I want to take a moment of silence to remember my loved ones who are now resting in paradise:

Grandma Gracie, Grandpa Big Hands, Uncle Levern, Cousin Tia Stoner...I miss y'all.

To my thugs from my Section, rest in paradise: Lil One (Angelo), MOD G (Ahmad Wilburn), Lucky, Mackie, Duck, Killa rob...you are forever in my memories.

To my fallen soldiers I met on my journey that have now passed away, rest in paradise: Lil Bud, Eddie BO, White Boi and Pretty Black.

To my loved ones: Mr. George Roberson, Granny, Ms. Diane Williams, Aunt Fern and Ratboy. May your souls rest in paradise... Forever in my heart.

And, to my Lil Brother Neal Da Peel aka Peezy... I love you brah...continue to embrace your blessings from God! Free my NapTown and Murder Muncie Thugs: Sundown, Dlove, White Mike, Buddy Love, Jerome Williams, T-Murder (Thomas Stokes),

Quanzay, Mann Ross and JRock (James Beasly). FREE MY BROTHERS!!!

A lot of people turned their backs on me throughout my journey. I forgive you, but the pain is too intense and won't allow me to forget. There are family members I'm so grateful for and I want to thank you: My Queen… I love you Mama! You will always be Queen. To my Grandma Cora, keep shining on me Sunshine. To my sister and best friend, I respect your hustle and you are now being passed the torch. Run wit it and secure the bag. To my Uncle McAdoo, you're the first man who really taught me the street hustle; gave me my first joint at five-years old ☺. I love you Unc. To my niece and my twin, love you Moonie!

To my Trill-ass cousins: Strictlybiz, Mar Atkins, T. Clay, Aaron Mason, Tytiana, Sweets, Pooh Jenkins, Tia Campbell, Tysheeda, Erica, Kendra, Cathy, Boone, Kudu, Anwar (Fudd), Godmom Cathy Rogers, Ms. Kim, Granny Barbara, Money Marc, Kareem, Nick Beam, King Papi, Ms. Doris, Trina (B.M.), Wifey Nisha, Sarah W., Sekia B, Thug Brah Coley and Lil Sis Deija, Pro (East Oakland 73rd Street)… If I forgot anyone, it's nuttin' personal. I'm not perfect. I'll catch you when I slide on the next one.

BULLETPROOF LOVE,
Philthy Phil

Sasha J. Special Thanks

I want to first thank God. Without Him none of this would be possible. I want to thank my beautiful Daughter for keeping me motivated; my Mom for giving me life and lacing me on how to be a Queen; my Grandma for teaching me the true value of life. To both my Brothers, without you two raising me and providing for me, where would I be? And to my Haters (supporters)… Motivate, don't hate… LOL… Y'all still ain't made it… Rest in heaven to my Grandma…

Sasha J

Contents

Certified Thrilla Part 3

CHAPTER 1

J erome helped Tameka into his Rover and he really felt sorry for her. The girl had been through a lot of shit lately and to make matters worse, they were both probably HIV positive. Jerome wasn't afraid of dying but he was definitely going to find out who killed his cousin.

"Yo', Meka, I apologize for earlier, shawty. I was out of pocket and I fucked up." Tameka began to cry again and shook her head. "Yo', let me see your phone. My phone is dead," he asked. She scrambled through all types of junk in her purse before she found her cell phone. Jerome took the phone and began to dial numbers. The phone continued to ring and he realized Nut probably didn't recognize the number. As he was about to click off, Nut answered his phone.

"Who dis?"

Jerome got straight to the point. "Listen my nigga, you know I been fucking with you since we was kids. I done always kept it real with you so I ain't 'bout to beat around the bush. When was the last time you seen or heard from C-Dollas before he died?"

Nut let the question marinate in his head for a while, wondering why Jerome was questioning him. But since he knew his homie was trying to get to the bottom of shit, he just overlooked his suspicions. "I told you nigga I was on top of that. Wasn't no need for you to even get all worked up, being you just came home and shit. But to keep it real, I hadn't talked to Keisha or C-Dollas for about a week prior to his death. I figured they was on some type of vacation and shit. You know that nigga be just bouncing and shit."

Jerome knew the nigga was full of shit and he didn't doubt one bit that Tameka was telling the truth. "Oh yeah, that's what's up. Damn, one mo' question, my nigga. I almost forgot. You sure C-Dollas wasn't 'pose to bring you his whip after you shot up shit at the hospital?"

The phone line was silent for about 20 seconds then the devil spoke. "I don't know Sherlock. You got all the answers. Maybe you should ask this bitch." Nut placed his cellphone up to Laneka's ear and she began rambling a thousand words a second.

"Baby, I'm sorry baby, I thought you was…"

Nut snatched the phone from her ear. "It seems like both of y'all been doing a little investigating. We can play this two ways. Either I can end this bitch's life or you can do it. You control her destiny."

Jerome couldn't believe his ears. What the fuck did Laneka have to do with anything and how the fuck did Nut know he was on to him? "Alright nigga, you win, you win. What is it that you want? I'm listening." Jerome had never been a coward nor had he ever put his life in danger for a bitch. But not only did he love Laneka, he knew Nut was a dangerous person. "Listen cuz, we done come too far to let some bitch come between us." Tameka looked at Jerome, startled at what he was saying as he continued to talk. "I think I already know why you flipped on C-Dollas and I don't blame you one bit. But what does La…"

Tameka snatched at her phone in a quick motion. She had a strange feeling something was wrong and her first instinct told her to call the police. She continued to grab at the phone from Jerome and it caused him to lose control of his truck just as the light turned red. Instead of stopping, he sped through the light and was T-boned on the right side of his truck by an 18-wheeler with a Coca Cola emblem on its side. The power and force of the semi-trailer threw the Range Rover 100 feet in the opposite direction and the Rover's left side collided with the bumper of a Ford Excursion, instantly releasing Jerome's airbag. As his face exploded with pain from the impact of the airbag, he could vaguely hear cars screeching to a stop and people yelling and talking in the background. He lifted his head and tried to gather his thoughts. Then he remembered he was not alone. The pain in his neck made it hard for him to turn to his right side but with all his willpower he managed to maneuver his body to the right.

The sight was gruesome and he thought he would throw up. Tameka's body had been twisted in such a way that her spine appeared broken. Her face was covered by a large amount of blood and she appeared to be dead. "Meka, Meka!" Jerome cried out in fear. Then he noticed a crowd of onlookers began to surround the truck and he started screaming, "Help! Help!" He inhaled a smell he could identify with his eyes closed — gasoline. He reached for his seatbelt which seemed to have jammed. Then Jerome heard someone yell words he was hoping not to ever hear.

"Y'all back up. The truck leaking gas and the engine looks like its smokin'. That muthafucka fenna blow!"

Jerome panicked and with all the energy he had left he pulled his key from the ignition. He always carried a Boy Scout pocket knife on his keychain equipped with a bottle opener and screw driver. He began to saw at the seatbelt strap as fast as he could. Finally, he was able to release himself from the straps of hell. He saw that he was trapped inside the truck and his only escape would be through the window beside Tameka which was shattered into pieces. He began to climb over her body.

"Look, that nigga ain't dead, he still alive!" some redneck shouted as Jerome lay half out the window. Then he heard a voice which would haunt him for the rest of his life.

"Rome, Rome, don't leave me like this, please! I...I...can't feel my legs. Rome, Ro..." Tameka cried out just as a pair of muscular arms reached around Jerome's upper body and pulled him out and towards the ground. As the man attempted to pull him away from the truck, Jerome protested.

"No! No, wait! My sister, she's still in the truck! Please help her!"

The man, who stood 6'7" and looked as if he weighed every bit of 300 pounds, carried Jerome 20 more feet away, telling onlookers not to touch him but wait on the ambulance. As he ran back to the truck he could see what appeared to be a dead woman facing away from him.

"Baby girl, baby girl," he whispered urgently as he ran to the truck. He reached for the door handle but it was of no use, damaged from the impact of the semi-trailer. As he reached through the window to release her seatbelt, he saw a flicker of flames licking the hood of the Rover. "Shit," he said as he began to panic because now the flames had engulfed the hood. He tried with all of his strength to release the "jaws of death" which had Tameka strapped and trapped inside of them.

"It's gone blow!" an onlooker screamed at him.

He had to choose between his life or the woman's life. "God, forgive me," he said out loud and then began running away from the truck like a mad man. He didn't get 15 feet away when he heard, BOOM! He knew the truck had exploded. The force of the explosion lifted him off his feet and threw him to the concrete. Jerome tried to regain his strength and lift himself off the ground. One of the bystanders stood over him talking.

"Be cool, man. The ambulance is on the way. Hang in there."

Jerome fell back onto the ground and mumbled, "Laneka…" and passed out.

* * * * * * * * *

Sergeant Lewis had been on his way home after a long day of work. He had finally made an impression on the Captain and since solving the string of hospital homicides he had been recommended for promotion to Lieutenant. He had enrolled himself into a private 12-step drug abuse program and since enrolling he had been clean for three weeks. Cherry had decided to walk out on him during his recovery and was still upset about the fact that no one had been arrested for the death of her sister and niece. Without Cherry in his life he was able to focus more on his job and less about pussy and crack.

As he prepared to take the right-away turn on Georgetown Road, he noticed a cloud of smoke and a large crowd of people standing around as if they were watching a freak show at a circus. He pulled his cruiser over to the side of the road and got out of the car.

"Over here officer, over here," a dark-skinned woman called out when she saw Sergeant Lewis hop out of his unmarked car. She had noticed his service revolver and his badge hanging around his neck and wondered why they sent only one cop and the ambulance still hadn't arrived. She could hear the sirens from the fire trucks and ambulance but had yet to see anyone. "Muthafuckas don't give two shits 'bout no niggas dying," she mumbled to herself before lighting a Newport menthol cigarette.

Sergeant Lewis ran over to the body sprawled out on the grass and once he saw the man' face, he had to restrain himself from committing murder. He knew this snitchin' nigga and he knew him well. He gritted his teeth and pretended to check for a pulse.

As he grabbed Jerome's wrist, he saw that two fire trucks had arrived and started to put out the blazing fire over the truck. An ambulance arrived shortly afterwards and the medics rushed to Jerome's aid. As two middle-aged EMT paramedic nurses lifted Jerome onto the stretcher he began to yell out Laneka's name. He became very violent and struck one of the nurses in the face.

"Strap him down, NOW!" the nurse yelled while holding his nose which was now bleeding. It took two uniformed officers to subdue Jerome while placing his wrists and legs in restraints. Afterwards they placed an oxygen mask over his nose and applied several I.V.'s to his arm. One I.V. contained a sedative that was used to calm mental patients. Within minutes of the injection Jerome was asleep and as harmless as a newborn baby. Sergeant Lewis watched them take Jerome away with murder in his heart.

* * * * * * * * *

"What the fuck is wrong with you? You sick bastard!" Laneka was trying to muster up some courage to save herself. She had always grown up fighting for Montana and Tameka and to her Nut was just a bully. She was duct-taped to a chair in her kitchen and could barely feel her hands because the tape was wrapped so tightly it had cut off her blood circulation.

Nut had been sitting on the couch, patiently waiting for Jerome to make his move. He didn't know if Jerome hung up on him intentionally or by mistake. But the fact that no one was answering the phone he had called from made him suspicious. He'd had enough of Laneka's mouth and he was at the point in his mind where he was just ready to merk the bitch. Even though he trusted Jerome and knew his nigga was solid, he knew pussy could change niggas' ways of thinking. It had been well over 45 minutes since he last spoke to Jerome and he wasn't about to sit around while Jerome made up his mind. Shit, for all he knew Jerome might have the SWAT Team on the way to surround the place. Nut made up his mind. If Jerome felt any aggression towards him about C-Dollas then fuck him; they would handle it in the streets.

"You just gone keep running that lil dick-sucker on yo' face until you can't talk no more, huh?" Nut walked over to Laneka and paced around her like a lion paces around its prey.

"What you gone do, kill me nigga? Just like you killed C-Dollas and like you killed them people at that house? I hope you rot in hell!"

Nut swung and caught her face with a vicious backhand that slapped all the taste out of her mouth.

Laneka started spitting large clots of blood out of her mouth and began laughing like a madwoman. "Ain't nothing you can do to hurt me. I've been to hell and back. But you know what's so fucked, you a real coward. You got me all tied up and shit like a lil ol' pussy. Here kitty, kitty. You ain't no killer, nigga. You'se an ol' coward."

Nut had heard enough. If her plan was to get to him she had succeeded. He walked around her once more and reached into his pants pocket and pulled out a black, handheld Taser and jammed it into the side of Laneka's neck, sending volts of electricity through her windpipe. Her body shook wildly as she began to foam from the mouth. Nut saw that she had passed out so he quickly cut the ropes off her and allowed her body to fall to the kitchen floor. As he sat there watching her regain consciousness he started laughing out loud.

"See what running yo' dick-sucker got you? Look at your dumb ass."

Laneka slowly moved her body and realized she was no longer restrained in a chair by ropes. She wondered what his madman plans were for her. Did he plan on raping her or letting her live? What was he thinking? "Listen, Nu…" Her throat felt like it was on fire and she gagged when she tried to talk. "Nut, I can pay you. Please just let me g…" She began to cough uncontrollably, but she managed to stand up and balance herself by holding onto the kitchen counter. Laneka wished she had the energy to reach for the knife that was on top of the stove but she was fatigued from the Taser attack.

Nut just looked at her as she stood up and balanced herself, wiping the foam from around her mouth with the back of her hand. "Now, now lil mama, exactly how much money you got?" Nut was curious. He knew Laneka lived a lavish lifestyle and from he and Jerome's prior conversations he knew she pushed a little weight in the city. "Speak up now. Don't be shy, I'm listening."

Laneka didn't trust him at all but she knew money could buy anything, even freedom. She had to risk it all. "I got over a $100,000 stashed in my wall safe in the closet in my room. The code is 31–19–27. Just let me go."

Nut couldn't believe his luck. This dumb bitch just paid him to do what he was gone do for free — kill her. "Let's go see about that," he told her, pulling out his .357 with the silencer on it. He shoved it into Laneka's back and marched her into her bedroom. He figured she probably had a gun in the safe and he'd give her a chance to reach for it.

Laneka walked over to her dresser and pushed it along the wall and sure enough a safe was behind where it once stood. She opened it and from where Nut stood at a distance, he could see the stacks of money. "It's all here, Nut. Just let me go."

Nut walked up behind Laneka. But as she quickly grabbed her loaded .45 from the safe Nut simultaneously put the .357 to her head. "Too slow," he laughed and splattered her brains all over the safe. As he collected the stacks of money and headed towards the front door, his attention was caught by a reporter on the TV who was reporting live from Georgetown Road where a three-truck crash had claimed the life of an unidentified black female. Paramedics and heroic citizen, Jamal Horn, were able to save Jerome Brown from the truck you see behind us which exploded.

The reporter asked, "What can you tell us, Mr. Horn?"

"Man, dude was trapped in his truck and shit and since I done took special training classes I knew I could save him. So I just ran over to the truck, jumped on the hood and used my fist to bust through the windshield," he exaggerated. "Then I ripped the seatbelt off him and carried him over there," he pointed. "But he kept saying something 'bout his sister being in the truck. So I run back over to the truck but before I could get close enough, it exploded," he lied. "I want to send shouts out to my mama, my baby-mama, and my baby-mama's mama. Oh yeah, and my CD's coming ou…" The camera shifted back to the reporter.

"Alright then, the police have the streets blocked off in the area for safety reasons so traffic may be backed up for several hours. As for the survivor, Jerome Brown, we've been told he is in stable condition at Wishard Hospital. Back to you Dan."

Nut had heard enough. He walked out the living room and into the kitchen and then headed for the front door. It was time for him to put the pieces of this puzzle together. He knew it would be hell trying to get in and out of the hospital since his last episode there. But this was Nut, the Certified Thrilla, and nothing was impossible.

CHAPTER 2

Desire Marrows aka "Diamond" had been introduced to the struggles of life at an early age. As she looked around her furnished house that she inherited after her mama passed away, she took a deep breath and thanked God she survived so many close encounters in life. Living in Atlanta, Georgia had its ups and downs. Now that she was no longer prostituting, stripping and boosting she had become accustomed to living life as a working-class woman. Years earlier she had been the victim of a brutal physical encounter with her ex-pimp that left her scarred for life and him without his life. The situation made her $20,000 richer and taught her many valuable lessons about life. Now working as a youth counselor in the West End district of Atlanta, she used this opportunity to reach out to other young black women who were being manipulated and forced into becoming sex objects for hire. She knew she couldn't save every teenager who came across her path, but she also knew if she could mentor and change one person's life, she could sleep easy, knowing she'd done her part.

Queen had received a mandatory 5-year sentence in Indiana's Women State Prison and on her release date she was met and greeted at the gate by Nut and Diamond. Nut agreed to help her get a new wardrobe and Diamond agreed that if Queen could get her parole transferred to Atlanta, she could stay with her. And since Diamond was in charge of everything at the West End Boys and Girls Club, she was able to craft and send a letter to the judge and parole board and convince them that by allowing Queen to relocate to Atlanta she could become a voice for the youth through sharing her experiences with them and other women. The parole board and judge promptly agreed.

For Diamond, that was the easy part of returning to Indiana; the hard part was facing Nut. He had grown, not only into a sexy individual, but he was still the respectable person she'd known him to be so many years ago. As bad as she wanted to feel him inside her again, she was too insecure with her own feelings to approach him. After getting her teeth repaired and several years of using Shea butter and Vaseline, her looks were restored to normal which made her a target for all the whistles and lame game that men ran. But that was the least of her worries. She was more concerned if Nut remembered what she used to do for a living and now that he was an adult, did he look down on her. Even as they hugged and caught up on lost time Diamond could sense that Nut had something bothering him but she never brought up what she was sensing. However, when she returned to Atlanta she cursed herself out for not at least telling him how she really felt.

It had been well over two years since the last time she saw Nut. Although they would call each other on holidays and send text messages they never once brought up any incidents from their pasts; not even their sexual escapade. As she snapped out of "memory lane" she heard keys at her front door. "Mama, is that you?" She got up and headed towards the door. After her biological mother passed away, Queen was the only motherly figure she had. Her father had been killed in a shootout by his own brother's gun when he accidently ran in front of him while they were shooting at their rivals. And as far as other family, that's just what they were — other family.

When Queen walked into the house she was carrying two Victoria Secrets bags and she sat them down by the door. She was greeted by Diamond with a kiss on the cheek as she closed the door behind her. "Hey baby, I wasn't gone but an hour. Did you miss this old woman?" she asked playfully and gave Diamond a hug. She walked over to a brown leather couch and sat down. "Girl, you wouldn't believe how many of them young niggas was jockin' an old lady like myself. Hell, I couldn't even go into Foot Locker and get a pair of running shoes they were hounding me so much," she said with a bit of coyness in her voice.

"Now mama, you know with all that ass hanging out them jeans and your hair whipped up like that, you look every bit of 21 or 22 years old," Diamond replied, laughing.

Queen kicked off her red-bottomed heels and laughed, too. Since transferring her parole here two years ago she had managed to earn an honest living. She had well over $170,000 in her bank account and was pushing a new Nissan Maxima on factory 20's. She was enrolled at a small community college studying for an Accounting degree. This would be her second degree. She had earned her first degree in prison and had a Bachelor's in Psychology. She was a certified Psychologist. She held group counseling meetings at the West End Boys and Girls Club on Thursdays and Saturdays and had her own office in downtown Atlanta off Peachtree Street where she had several celebrity clients she counseled and acted as their personal advisor. She charged anywhere between $300.00 to $500.00 dollars per hour. Some sessions could last up to five hours, depending on who it was; such as the ex-NBA player who liked to cross-dress and wear tongue rings and was one her most lucrative clients.

"I'm so tired of these tired-ass niggas. Girl, it's pitiful. My old ass need to find a working man who can play Sugah Daddy."

Diamond laughed at Queen's comment. She knew any nigga who fucked with Queen had to have twice as much as she had to put up with her jazzy attitude. Prison had made her wiser and given her a heart of concrete when it came to bullshit. "Shit, all them damn Hollywood stars you give therapy to, I'm sure you can get all inside their heads."

Queen rolled her eyes and grabbed a pack of Newport cigarettes on the table. She shook the pack then crumbled it up and threw it at Diamond. "Yo' funky ass done smoked all my 'ports. I knew I should've took 'em with me."

Diamond started smiling and reached underneath the couch and threw a fresh pack on the table. "Ha! I got your old ass."

Queen rolled her eyes again and grabbed the pack, quickly ripping it open. As she fired up a Newport 100 and inhaled her cellphone started ringing. She fumbled through her purse and found it and tapped "talk." She got up and walked towards her bedroom and Diamond became curious. It wasn't just that she went into another room to talk; it was the look on her face after her first 15 seconds on the phone. Diamond started to get up and ask her if something was wrong but decided not to invade her privacy. Five minutes later, Queen walked slowly back into the living room.

"Diamond, oh baby, the devil sho' does work in mysterious ways. It's Nut. He's in trouble and he needs us." Queen walked over to the couch and sat back down and lowered her head into the palm of her hands.

"What is it mama? Is he hurt, is he in jail, I mean what's so important? Talk to me, dammit!" Diamond became frustrated. She had always vowed to be there for Nut, no matter what the situation. But now that she had matured and established herself as a role model, she didn't feel as if she could hold onto that promise any longer and not jeopardize her career.

"Get some sleep. We jumping on the highway in the morning, baby." She grabbed the pack of Newports off the table and walked into her bedroom.

Diamond sat up all night, stressing about what could possibly be going on. She thought about calling Nut herself and confronting him but knew going behind Queen's back would only cause problems. Before she closed her eyes in sleep, she said a brief prayer and asked the Lord to protect her and lead her not into destruction and deliver her from temptations and evildoings. She just knew whatever was going on in Indiana was serious and once she got on the highway there was no turning back. "Maybe things ain't as serious as I think," she whispered to herself as she drifted off to sleep.

CHAPTER 3

J oshua Ruckford grew up living the life any white kid from the suburbs would live. As a child he was fortunate enough to have two parents who worked and provided for him and his brother. He graduated with honors from high school and received a full scholarship to play football at Norte Dame. After blowing out his knee in spring training, his football career was dimmed and he lost all motivation to continue school. And moving back in with his parents hadn't been as easy as it had been when he was a youth. They were disappointed with him quitting college and vowed not to pacify him any longer. He would have responsibilities now that he was an adult and the first one was to get a job and save enough money to get his own place.

His father had been the Chief Medical Examiner for Wishard Hospital and had been able to convince the supervisor in Human Resources to give his son a job as a part-time security guard. So, after an interview, background check and physical Joshua was hired. He got in good with everyone there and he became the head guy around the hospital premises. He got his brother and best friend a job, too. To him, the job couldn't have been easier. All you had to do was circle the parking lot in the company jeep every hour, monitor the waiting room and check the bathroom stall every 12 hours.

Joshua had earned himself the nickname "Too Tall" because of his height and size. Even though his appearance might have intimidated loiters, all the hospital staff knew he had a gentle and loving soul. He would run small errands for the nurses and talk to the little kids who would come into the waiting room with the flu, broken limbs or minor injuries. He was the life of the waiting room. Sometimes when things were slow he would go into the Starbucks across the street and order a Cappuccino. Working together with his brother and friend they would sometimes rotate positions. Joshua would monitor the parking lot while his brother stood watch over the waiting room and his best friend would go to every floor and monitor visitors and make sure the "no cellphones – no smoking" rules were enforced. One minute you'd see Josh in the waiting room and the next minute you'd see his brother. They basically did what they wanted to do whenever they wanted to do it. They were dubbed "The 3 Musketeers." When people became violent or junkies roamed around the premises, they would handle the situation without conflict. There had been no serious incidents that resulted in an arrest since they had been security guards at the hospital.

But all that changed the day he came face-to-face with the madman he would remember for the rest of his life. Not only did the monster take the life of his brother and best friend, but he was still out there hiding somewhere like a coward. Josh felt responsible for the death of his brother and best friend. If only he hadn't asked his brother to fill in for him while he ran over to Starbucks to get a drink and check his Facebook page on the internet service they provided. His brother would be alive today. When Josh first encountered Nut in the Emergency waiting room he could tell the guy was hot-headed but figured all black people had anger problems. If he would have stayed a while longer his brother would still be here. As security guards they weren't allowed to carry firearms but Joshua played by his own rules and always kept a .380 automatic in a holster strapped to his ankle just in case. He had been to several shooting ranges and could hit moving targets from the chest area to the cranium. He would regret leaving his brother for the rest of his life. So after talking to a black detective and being forced to identify C-Dollas as the hospital shooter, he knew he would have to take matters into his own hands.

After doing some investigation of his own he found out Keisha Jones did in fact have a brother. He convinced his father that the person who killed his brother was still out there, roaming the streets. So his father obtained Keisha Jones' hospital records which detailed information back to her date of birth. Not only did it list all immunization shots, checkups and hospital visits, but it listed her mother, father, siblings, an uncle in Atlanta and her brother, Lester Jones. After obtaining her brother's hospital records he was also able to obtain a medical release of confidential records and traced the address to a group home outside of Indianapolis. The group home had requested Lester's medical records for the nursing staff to keep on file; so Joshua now had evidence to prove Keisha Jones had a brother.

After calling several group homes and talking to counselors he was informed that as a juvenile Lester ran away from home and when he was apprehended he was sentenced to the Department of Corrections. Joshua knew this was public information and after he hung up the phone he went online. After gaining access to the Indiana Department of Corrections (I.D.O.C.) website, he typed in Lester's full name. Ten matches appeared with different dates of birth. After looking through the hospital file he found Lester's date of birth and typed it in, waiting for what seemed like minutes. The file popped up and the image of a young Lester Jones filled his Apple computer screen. He became overwhelmed with rage. Even though the picture was over ten years old, Lester's face hadn't changed that much. Joshua broke down into tears.

He reached for his cellphone to call Detective Lewis but stopped as he told himself "all black people stick together." So he decided to surf the internet to try and find a physical address for Lester. After hours of this, he almost gave up. And just as he was about to shut down his computer, something told him to Google the phrase, "Lester Jones, runaway" and the newspaper article detailing the arrests of Queen and Lester Jones came up. He searched the I.D.O.C. website again and found out Queen had been paroled two years ago. It was too late to contact the parole office and get an address for her or for Lester, so he printed out all the information he had found on the computer before shutting it down. He got up from his desk and walked into his bedroom closet and pulled out a black duffel bag. He slowly unzipped it before reaching inside. He took the SKS-47 out the bag and looked at it then stood up. He walked over to a wall and looked at the framed picture of his brother and his best friend in the hospital's parking lot smiling, with their arms slung across each other's shoulders. He kissed the picture and said, "I'm my brother's keeper."

* * * * * * * * *

Nut paced back and forth in the living room of his small hideaway studio apartment. It had been months since he stepped foot into the apartment and used it for emergencies only. No one knew where it was located; not even Jerome. When Nut needed to gather his thoughts, this is where he would run to. He walked into his kitchen thinking to himself that he needed a change of lifestyle. Since Keisha passed away, everything he did became personal. He put together a blueprint in his head and prayed Queen and Diamond would come through for him. After calling the hospital several times he was aware of Jerome's progress and knew it wouldn't be long before he checked himself out, therefore, capable of popping up at any moment. It would probably take Queen at least nine hours to drive from Atlanta to

Indianapolis and if everything fell into place they would be in and out of the hospital before anyone knew what happened.

Nut knew he couldn't go into the hospital, especially if Jerome had diarrhea of the mouth and told anything to the detectives. His best chance of getting close to Jerome was through Queen and Diamond. Not only did Jerome not know who they were, they were going to pose as Laneka and Tameka's family members. Nut was a mastermind at plots and disguises and this was his kind of game. He had already figured that Jerome didn't know any of Laneka's family other than the Uncle who played "Inspector Gadget" on one occasion. This was going to be easy. Although, he'd had second thoughts about carrying out his plan but he knew he had to eliminate Jerome. Jerome wasn't a pushover but he wasn't built for this war shit. But Jerome would either put him behind bars or disappear and fight him another day. Nut just couldn't take that chance. He knew Jerome would never forgive him for the death of Laneka and Jerome would definitely want to retaliate for the death of C-Dollas, even if it meant going to the detectives.

Nut picked up his phone and set the alarm for 5:30 a.m. He would call Queen and make sure they were headed his way and if so they could be in town by 3:00 p.m. this afternoon. He wanted to have a clear mind about everything. As he walked back into the living room and lay on the sofa, he closed his eyes and said a small prayer. "Lord, forgive me for what I've done and what I'm about to do. You know my heart and you know my situations. What I'm really trying to say is..." and Nut dozed off in the middle of his prayer and drifted off into thug's paradise.

* * * * * * * * *

As Diamond rolled over, her limbs tangled in her satin sheets, she was awakened from a wet dream. "Fuck!" Her cellphone was ringing off the hook. She could tell by her Michael Jackson ringtone, "I'll Be There," it was important. She looked at her phone and saw it was the faculty director at the Boys and Girls Club. "Hey...what's going o... damn, what time is it anyway?" She pulled the phone from her ear and looked at the clock on its blue screen.

"Sorry to wake you up at this time Ms. Marrows but this is an urgent matter concerning one of the girls in your case load. I'm sure you already know who we're talking about."

Diamond lifted herself up on an elbow. It was 4:40 a.m. in the morning. She knew she and Queen had to be on the highway in a couple of hours. She didn't have time for this. "What has Star done this time? Don't tell me she and her mama's boyfriend got into it again."

Diamond had been a Big Sister role model for Star, who was a 13-year old ex-prostitute who had been exposed to crack cocaine and turned out into the streets of Atlanta. She had been arrested several times for shoplifting, solicitation and consumption of alcohol by a minor. For the past couple of months she had been complaining about the way her mother's boyfriend had been acting towards her since she returned home. She said she felt uncomfortable being home alone with him. Since returning home she had been clean of crack cocaine but stated that he offered her weed and beer from time to time.

She admitted that one day when she was getting dressed she felt eyes on her as if she was being watched and moments later she noticed the bushes outside her bedroom window were moving. She never left her curtains open but she saw that today they were pulled open enough to allow a peep show. But she couldn't prove anything. And on another occasion when she went to get on the computer and check her Facebook messages, her mother's boyfriend had forgotten to log off the website and he had been on the site "Barely Legal XXX" and the scenes disgusted her. She had always felt he was a pervert but her mama always defended him. So now, when Diamond ended her questions, the director pierced her heart with bad news.

"Not only did they get into it but Star claims he got drunk and tried to rape her. Diamond, she sliced up the man's face with a box cutter and he's in critical condition because of the loss of blood."

Diamond couldn't believe what she had just heard. She remembered one day when she suspected Star of using crack and as she rummaged through her purse she found a metal box cutter. After confiscating it and throwing it away, Diamond figured Star would get another one. This was a troubled teenager.

"So where is Star being held and what is she charged with?" Diamond hoped it wasn't attempted murder. She actually prayed it wasn't. As she waited for the response she walked over to her closet, looking for something comfortable to slip into.

"Diamond, she's with me. She left the scene of the crime and called me from her cellphone, screaming and yelling that she had killed someone. I made her call her mother, who at the time all this happened, had her stank ass in the club. Her mama said the police had put out a warrant for her arrest and if she caught Star first she was going to 'kill the little bitch'."

Star had snatched the phone from the director and rambled off 100 words per second. "I didn't do it! I mean I told y'all he was a sick bastard! That bitch-ass nigga tried to rape me while I was sick but I always keep my box cutter under my pillow because

I knew he would come when my mama ain't there. It ain't my fault, Diamond! I swear! You believe me, don't you?"

Diamond started crying as she slipped on a pair of jeans. She grabbed her coat and headed for the front door. "Don't worry, baby. I'm on my way. Where y'all at? Put Susan back on the phone. It ain't yo' fault, you hear me? We gone get to the bottom of this." Diamond walked over to the table and scribbled a quick note to Queen asking her to call her when she got up. She knew Queen hated to be awakened before her time to get up. Plus, this was personal.

Still on the phone, Susan said, "We at the Waffle House on Metropolitan Avenue. We sitting in the back. Hurry up."

Diamond walked out the door and got into Queen's Nissan Maxima and headed to the Waffle House. She couldn't let lil sis go through this alone. She hoped Queen wouldn't be mad about her taking her car, but she had no other option because her Magnum was in the repair shop. Queen would just have to understand.

* * * * * * * * *

Nut's cellphone alarm went off and made him jump up and clutch his .357, aiming it in all directions. "Damn, it's 5:30 all fucking ready. Shit," he mumbled to himself. He walked into the bathroom and took a piss. After flushing the toilet he walked over to the sink to wash his hands. He ran his wet hands over his face and reached for a towel hanging on a rod to dry it off. He rubbed the towel down his face and opened his eyes and saw the letters MBK written in blood on the bathroom mirror. "MBK...what the fuck?" he whispered. Then an image appeared out of nowhere behind him in the mirror which fucked his head up.

"Yeah, MBK, my brother's keeper. But in this case, my bitch Laneka!" and Jerome emptied the clip into Nut's back as he stood over him reloading and unloading, reloading and unloading. Nut felt every bullet. Then Nut's cellphone started ringing and woke him up again, realizing that after he turned off his alarm the first time, he'd fallen back asleep. Now he had overslept and the clock read 6:15 a.m. He'd just had another fucked up dream and this time it was so real he'd felt it; even washing up in the bathroom felt real. He looked at the Caller ID and saw it was Queen.

"Yo', where y'all at? Y'all on the highway or what?"

Queen had just awakened and realized Diamond was gone. After reading the note she had left and calling her she understood the situation. But what she didn't understand was why Diamond hadn't awakened her. Now she was stranded with no wheels and only two cigarettes left. "Baby, something came up. I'm sorry, I'm so sorry. I ain't even got my car. I don't even know how to explain this shit."

Nut wanted to crush his phone. When everybody needed him he was always there. Now when he needed one fucking favor Queen couldn't come through. "You know what? Fuck it! I don't need y'all anyways. Y'all a just hold me up. I'm gone." Nut pressed END and cut off the call.

Queen didn't realize Nut was no longer there and said, "I love you baby. Be careful and I'll be there." There was no response. "Hello, hello…" She looked at her phone and saw that the call had been terminated.

CHAPTER 4

"Now tell me this again. You say this guy, Nut, is responsible for the hospital massacre and several other homicides, is that correct?" Sergeant Lewis stood over Jerome in his hospital bed as he supplied the detective the most refreshing information he had heard since he'd been on the force.

"Listen man, I'm telling you, if you don't get over to my girl's crib he gone kill her! Dude's on some other shit. How many times I got to fuckin' tell you, he gone kill my girl! Fuck!!" Jerome tried to get out of the hospital bed but was quickly slammed down by Sergeant Lewis.

Lewis pulled out his revolver and shoved it into Jerome's cheek. "Where the fuck you think you going, huh? Now you listen and you listen good, nigga. Until I sort this shit out, you ain't going nowhere." Sergeant Lewis looked over his notes and made sure he had Laneka's address on his pad. He called the rookie officer standing outside the room. "Santiago, cuff this fucker up and make sure no one visits him. I don't care if it's his damn mama. The only ones permitted in here are the doctors and nurses. If this fucker even breathes wrong, book him for vehicular homicide and have him transported to county jail. I'm sure they'd love to know a snitch is in the dorm, huh Jerome?" Lewis left the room and Santiago followed his orders while Jerome worried about Laneka. Jerome was also puzzled that Sergeant Lewis hadn't brought up their prior relationship. But if Lewis didn't mention it, he sure as hell wasn't going to mention it.

* * * * * * * * *

Joshua Rockford had been on the highway for seven hours. After speaking with the parole office and faxing them bogus and altered hospital forms to support his claim that he needed the address of a patient who came in for a biopsy and wanted to get the results to her. The young operator transferred him to someone who not only provided him with Queen's employment address but her current residence. He had been up all night drinking water and snorting crystal meth to keep him up and alert. He had stopped six different times since leaving Indiana to refill his 32 ounce cup with coffee, no sugar, no cream, just black, John Wayne coffee — mud. His intentions were not to hurt anyone but only to bring this psychotic killer to justice. And if that meant harming someone, then deep inside he was prepared to deal with the consequences of his actions.

After crossing the state line into Georgia he activated his navigational screen in his new Ford Explorer and proceeded to travel straight to his destination with no stops. Nothing or anyone was going to keep him from the truth. He was now the hunter and Lester was the prey. Then he contacted his friend Johnathan Allen.

* * * * * * * * *

As Jerome sat in his hospital bed he knew there was no turning back. He had done the unthinkable, again: snitched, squealed, rolled over, and spilled the beans. He had broken the code of the streets. He never asked himself why. He just kept consoling himself by repeating silently, "I got a life. I got to think about my girl and she don't deserve this shit. It's my fault. Nut shouldn't have forced my hand. I mean, shit, I'm a real nigga protecting his girl. Fuck what niggas think. A nigga ain't gone understand unless he in my shoes." And, he refused to even think about Tameka right now. He was eaten up with guilt whenever he did. God, how was he going to tell Laneka about her sister? So he continued watching "Magnum P.I." on the 17" Panasonic hospital TV and eventually dozed off. When he next opened his eyes he saw his room was still under guard by that fuckin' rookie cop. The fuckin' pig-ass crooked muthafucka needed to go get the real criminals. But as much as he hated the police he felt safe because he knew Nut, and Nut was worse than anyone's nightmares. If he went to hell, Nut could give Lucifer nightmares. Jerome was in deep shit.

Just as Jerome closed his eyes a second time and fell into a light sleep, he was awakened by a disturbing noise. He opened his eyes and looked to his left. He released a deep breath because it was only the janitor coming into the room to change the trash bag and wipe down the bathroom with disinfectant. Jerome hated feeling paranoid.

"Aye, O.G. you think you can grab the TV remote from off the floor for me. These punk-ass pigs got a brother cuffed up." The janitor who had his back to Jerome mumbled a couple of words before replacing the white hefty trash can with a new trash bag. As he continued to perform his tasks Jerome became frustrated. "Damn nigga, you too good to look out for a muthafucka just like the rest of these backward-ass Uncle Tom's?" Jerome tried rolling over into a more comfortable position while adjusting the bed.

When the janitor completed what he was doing he walked over to the Universal remote on the floor and picked it up with his latex covered hand and tossed it onto Jerome's stomach. He headed to the bathroom mumbling to himself about "people having no respect."

Jerome caught the butt-end of the janitor's comment and couldn't help adding his two cents worth. "Nigga, you just like an 'ol slave, still cleaning up for the white man. Yeah, clean that piss and shit out the toilet you ol' miserable scumbag." Jerome didn't really mean what he was saying but he was upset and frustrated about the position he was in.

As the janitor pulled the bathroom door slightly closed and turned on the water, he began to whistle a familiar tune. He unbuttoned the third and fourth buttons on his hospital issued janitor's shirt and drew out a loaded .357 with a silencer attached to it. "Yeah, all you young street punks is just alike. Y'all truce breakers, backstabbers and tender dick for these hoes," the janitor yelled from behind the bathroom door.

Suddenly, Jerome's brain recognized the voice coming from behind the door but it was too late. The door swung open and Jerome looked into the eyes of Satan in the flesh — Nut. Jerome yelled out to the officer who was supposed to be seated outside in front of the room. "Aye! Yo' cop! Help! Aye man, can't you hear me?" What Jerome didn't know was that Nut had broken the young officer's neck in two places with one twist. Hospital staff, patients and others passing by just thought the young officer was tired and exhausted, taking a few winks on the job. "Goddammit the fuckin' killer's in the room! Don't you fuckin' hear me, copper? Fuck!"

Nut walked over to Jerome and shook his head. "They say what's done in the light comes to the dark, or is it the other way around? Anyways, let's look at the brighter side of things. Today is your last day living on this shit we call earth. I loved you like a brother. I would've given you my left lung so you could breathe and you fuckin' crossed me, you goddamned snake!" Nut had fire in his eyes but he also had tears. But as much as it hurt him, he knew Jerome had to die. "C-Dollas was a fag, a homosexual trying to play the role of a Casanova/street hustler. He fucked up and stuck his dick in the wrong woman which was my sister, so I smoked him. You satisfied? Yo' nosey-ass bitch put herself in a situation she had nothing to do with. Oh, what the hell. Why am I explaining myself? Open yo' mouf' Jerome."

Jerome just kept mumbling the word, "Why?" with guilt, pain and tears in his eyes. He began to whimper like a kid. "Come on Nut, all we got is us brah. Fuck C-Dollas. He knew he was wrong. And Laneka, shit I ain't even know the bitch like that. It's all 'bout us. I been riding for you since day one." Nut pulled the hammer back on the .357 and started to squeeze.

"I wouldn't do that if I was you Mr. Lester Jones, or is it Nut?"

Jerome couldn't believe his eyes. The Lord was with him today. Sergeant Lewis stood behind Nut, pointing his .40 caliber at the back of Nut's head.

A thousand different things ran through Nut's mind and he had to make a decision quickly. As he stood there looking into Jerome's eyes he noticed a smirk on Jerome's face and right then and there Nut didn't give a fuck. He had made up his mind; Jerome was dying with him.

"It's like this Nut, I could splatter your goddamned brains all over this room and it would be justifiable homicide, open-shut case. You killed the damn burrito I had guarding the room and this little singing-ass pussy you came for is gone get on the stand and sing like Luther Vandross. Ain't that right, Jerome?"

Jerome rolled his eyes and wished the Sergeant would just hurry up and get it over with. Sergeant Lewis told Jerome that he'd had a feeling Nut would come to the hospital. Lewis just didn't think Nut was this clever. He had underestimated him. "But listen Nut, today is your lucky day. I got bigger fish to fry. So drop your weapon and do what I tell you."

Nut knew that he could easily kill Jerome but how he could avoid a bullet in his head was another story. Nut put his hands in the air and surrendered. Lewis took the revolver from his hand.

"Nice silencer. Let's see if it really works." He squeezed the trigger twice, hitting his target in the chest. "Bulls eye."

CHAPTER 5

Queen sat on the loveseat in the living room of her crib, puffing on a Newport. For the last few hours she had been frustrated and under complete stress because Diamond had left her with no vehicle during a very drastic moment. She smashed her last Newport in the ashtray and thought about calling Nut again to explain what was going on to him. As she stood up to grab her cellphone off the kitchen counter she noticed a dark shadow through the off-white curtains that hung at the window next to the front door. Queen was no fool. Her prison instincts told her something was not right about this picture.

She slowly walked to the kitchen and grabbed her cellphone. Then in three large steps made her way to the kitchen refrigerator where she slowly opened the stainless steel door and pulled out an orange box of Arm and Hammer baking soda. She shoved her hand in the box and when she withdrew it her hand was clutching a .22 semi-automatic covered in baking soda. Again, she was no fool. She kept her weapon stored there because parole was liable to pop up at any time. But she could sense this was no damn parole; not snooping around the front door. She contemplated calling the authorities but she did not want to come into contact with the law.

She took a deep breath and gained the courage to walk to the front door. She intended to surprise whoever was outside. But before she got to the door the shadow moved and there was a knock. Who the fuck could it be? Queen put her eye to the peephole. Damn, it was the police. She tucked the gun in her waistband underneath her shirt then she opened the door.

It was Joshua in his security uniform. "Hello," he said then sprayed her in the face with mace as he entered the house.

CHAPTER 6

"For a minute, I thought you was gone smoke my black ass," Nut said as he reclined in his La-Z-Boy, eating a bowl of Captain Crunch Berries cereal. He had his feet kicked up as he wiggled his toes, watching sports highlights on ESPN.

"Nigga, I told you a long time ago to let me handle this shit. In the end we all come out on top," Sergeant Lewis said as he got up and grabbed the burning blunt out the ashtray.

"Naw, naw I ain't never doubt your plan. I just didn't want no other officers talking to Jerome's rat ass. That would of really put me in the fuckin' spotlight." Nut turned the TV down and leaned toward Sergeant Lewis. "So you been really holding a grudge since Jerome got on the stand and told the jury that you set up the whole kidnapping charge he caught a while back?"

Lewis never went into detail about what happened but he felt that Nut was more than trustworthy. "Yeah, the sucka tried to burn me. I mean Jerome had always been one of my ears to the street. When I worked in the Narcotics Task Unit I would be the first to know about all the top priority raids and dealers. I would then give this information to Jerome and let him run up into somebody's spot and lay 'em down before we got a chance to hit. I mean, who would you rather lose yo' money to — a street punk you can seek revenge on or a "by-the-book rookie cop?"

Nut shook his head in agreement.

"Anyhow, I had this young kid named Oscar on the payroll. He would give me a large amount of money every month for information I had on raids. He would inform other dealers and collect money from them for the information. It was all good until the fucker tried to side-cross me. I found out through one of my little "birds" on the street that Oscar was planning on packing up and moving out the country." Lewis could tell he had Nut's attention. "Well, to make a long story short I sent Jerome to collect "rent money" from the sucka. But while Jerome was duct-taping the nigga and shit, the damn feds ran up in the middle of it all. They'd had Oscar under surveillance the whole damn time and of course, me being an officer, the Feds ain't sharing no information with my department."

Nut kept listening intently.

"Anyhow, the feds couldn't pick up the case on Jerome because it wasn't a drug buy and Oscar was not a federal agent or paid informant. So the state picked up the case. Jerome got on the stand and tried to take down the force. However, because of insufficient evidence, all charges against me were dropped. But Internal Affairs knew I was dirty and sent me straight to Homicide. They figured if they put me in a position such as Sergeant of Homicide I would fuck up, have large case loads of unsolved murders and then they would fire me. It's all politics, trust me." Lewis took a deep breath. "So when Jerome saw me at the hospital he thought that seven years made a difference and that I would just forgive his snitchin' ass. I fed his ass, took him in on my team and told him not to cross me." Lewis became angry just thinking about it. "But let's discuss this brick wall in our way. You ever heard of Captain Smith?"

CHAPTER 7

It was a very hot day and it was humid in the precinct located downtown off Market Street. Several officers had personal mini-fans attached to their desks because maintenance had yet to fix the problem in the building's A/C blower. Sergeant Lewis sat at his desk and completed a crossword puzzle in the back of the newspaper. He was exhausted from dealing with paperwork associated with Jerome's death which brought the hospital massacre death toll to eight. After hours of questioning and interviews with Internal Affairs, it was determined by his superiors that the suspect from the first murders was still alive and Sergeant Lewis had not satisfied the department with the investigation he had done.

He knew he was getting sloppy. He was unable to cover up his tracks and just when he thought he had all the answers there were more questions. He knew fooling with Nut was like treading in an ocean full of sharks, but he had become desperate. After doing his own investigation he found out that Keisha actually did have a brother and through the streets he also found out that Nut was a "hothead," a "psychopath," a "headbusta." After the security guard at the hospital kept telling Lewis what he already knew, he just figured he'd track Nut down and put it all on the table. "Roll with me or roll against me and if you roll against me, you get rolled over, point blank."

Nut figured he could kill two birds with one stone. He would get any evidence against him destroyed and in the end show Sergeant Lewis who was smarter.

As Lewis sat lost in his thoughts, he was shaken out of his daydream by a voice he hated. "Yo' Lewis! Front and center." It was the Captain so he definitely had to go.

CHAPTER 8

Special Federal Agent Mondo Taroski had been in the field for 12 years. He had seen it all: murder, extortion, conspiracy, racketeering, embezzlement, you name it. His status at the J. Edgar Hoover Building was that of a "hotshot." He had solved 85% of his cases and had never lost a case once it went to trial and presented before a jury. For the past eight years he would lose sleep thinking about the one person he dreamed of nailing: Steve Lewis; Sergeant Steve Lewis. He knew this was a dirty cop. He knew Lewis was as dirty as they came and if there was one thing he hated, it was someone who abused the badge.

Growing up in Germany had been rough for Mondo. His grandparents were killed during the Holocaust by Hitler. But after his father successfully smuggled the family to America, things got worse for him. The kids in America were mean. They would laugh at Mondo's clothing, joke about his name and knock his Jewish cap off his head. From that date forward he vowed to fight the "bad people." He studied hard in school and graduated top of his class. He enrolled in college and studied criminal justice. Not satisfied with the law and the grimy streets of Indianapolis, he joined the police Academy. The instructor—who was also a German Jewish Holocaust survivor—noticed rare skills in Mondo and referred him to the Federal Agent Academy. He passed all background, immigration and physical skills test. He was now finally somebody. He had worked hard for everything he had. Nothing was given to him on a silver platter. He would not rest again until Steve Lewis was buried under city hall.

His beef with Sergeant Lewis started like usual beefs start; in the streets. Mondo felt Lewis destroyed a perfect open and shut case he had been building against Oscar Sanchez. With orders from his superiors he allowed Oscar to continue his legal activities until there was enough evidence to put him away under a mandatory life sentence. Mondo's instincts told him to go over his superior's head. But being the model officer he was he followed all procedures. Sergeant Lewis had not only thrown a screwball into Mondo's case, he had dishonored the gold badge he wore on his chest. He was a disgrace to the justice system. He was one of the "bad people."

After weeks, months and long stressful hours, Agent Mondo Taroski got the break he was looking for. Not only did Jerome Brown get on the stand and spill the beans, but after finally convicting Oscar of manufacturing and distributing crack cocaine he was able to convince Oscar to give up his supplier. But after thinking things through more thoroughly, Oscar decided not to turn on his family and instead, he gave vivid details about Sergeant Lewis' involvement while he was head of the Narcotics Task Unit. He babbled on and on about how his family were poor immigrants from Mexico and how he met Steve Lewis. He said Lewis threatened to deport his family to Mexico if Oscar refused to sell large amounts of drugs for him. He broke down in tears while telling Mondo of nights without a decent meal on the table. He explained to the agent that it was either do as he was told and sell the drugs to feed his family and enjoy the freedoms of America, or lose his chance to get a piece of the American Dream and go back to Mexico, working in sweat shops for pennies. He stated, "I had no choice."

Oscar looked Mondo directly in the eyes during the three-hour interview and said something that crumbled Mondo's heart. "You look at me. What you see, pig? You t'ink I sell coca to buy fancy wardrobe? You t'ink I sell yaeyo to purchase big mansion? If this what you t'ink, let me tell you this supacop, me had no chance. Me family no wanna live day-to-day eating beans and flour tortillas. You look at me peoples like we contaminate yo' country but look at yo' country. You gringos and negroes too proud to flip a beef pattie cause you t'ink that's for lower class people. You too lazy to do the house cleaning in yo' big mansions. Then who you hire? Us. We flip the burgers, work as maids and do the dirty work just to live in yo' country. Do we complain about minimum wage? No, cause to us it's 10 times more than we used to, but you still look down on us. Then you scream we taking all the jobs. You t'ink every Mexican jump the border with 10 kilos and thirty pounds of marijuana, huh? You ever slept in a house built out of clay wit no air conditioning system in the middle of July with a house full of cousins, uncles, aunties and lil kids crying? You ever been laughed at cause you talk different or because you have no money, huh tuff guy? I'm not your problem. Go look in the mirror. Me not selling the yaeyo for me, me selling the yaeyo for you; for my family to have a decent life; and you call this the land of the free."

Mondo's face turned blood-red as he reached across the table to grab Oscar by the collar of his federal issued jumpsuit. He looked him in the eyes and whispered two words: "I know."

* * * * * * * * *

After weeks of convincing the DA's office of Sergeant Lewis' involvement, the DA agreed to give Oscar a "time served" sentence in exchange for his recorded, written and physical testimony during trial. Mondo had apologized to Oscar and told him his life story. They were both shocked to find out they had so much in common. Mondo agreed to help Oscar get a job as a paid federal informant. He explained to him the importance of getting the "bad people" off the streets. He also told him that what he was doing would help America look at his race differently instead of as gate jumpers, boarder hoppers and drug smugglers. But the day Oscar was supposed to be released, he was found in the shower with his penis cut off and shoved in his mouth and a mop handle shoved up his anus with the word "Rat" carved on his forehead with a razorblade. Since there were no cameras in the shower it was impossible to say who was responsible.

Agent Taroski personally interviewed each of the 200 inmates in the unit and after several threats of new charges, including the death penalty, the only thing each inmate said was, "You seen what happened to him for opening his mouth. You think I wanna die like that?"

Mondo didn't even try to perform any further investigation after that. He already knew he would put this blood on Sergeant Lewis' hands.

* * * * * * * * *

Mondo lost a lot of sleep, not to mention weight, and even the desire to date. He conducted off-duty surveillance on Lewis and had over 300 photo shots of him. He had pictures of Cherry and after a background check found out she was a stripper. He would use his inside resources to reopen cases Lewis had been assigned to. He would spend hours trying to find loopholes in any of Lewis' investigations that could prove a cover-up.

He was resting his head on his cherry wood computer desk and was shaken out of his deep thoughts when his cellphone started ringing. He picked it up and answered gruffly, "What!"

"Now is that any way to speak to your partner?" the caller asked.

Mondo became alert. This was the call he had been waiting on. After several weeks of researching the hospital murders, including the death of Jerome Brown, all the dots connected and spelled LEWIS. Not only was he the lead detective throughout the case but he failed to follow leads and follow-up on statements made by several eyewitnesses. But after receiving an email from one of the security guards who had seen the actual suspect, Mondo decided to follow-up on the email. The email was filled with a photo of Nut, his background history and notes explaining his connection to the hospital massacre. After further research, Mondo wasn't even surprised to learn that Jerome—the same Jerome who was involved in Oscar's case, Lewis' scandal and other criminal activities—was the same Jerome mysteriously murdered along with an officer. And guess who the lead detective was that found the bodies? Exactly; Sergeant Lewis. But Mondo continued to perform extensive research and found out this Nut character and Jerome were like brothers. Even though his instincts told him this was something bigger than he'd ever seen, he still didn't have the missing piece to the puzzle. Who exactly was Nut? Where did he fit into all of this mayhem? And what was his and Sergeant Lewis' involvement with each other? Mondo turned his attention back to his call.

"What you got for me, Josh?" he asked calmly.

"Oh, I think it's not what I got but who I got," Josh replied, laughing sarcastically. Then he explained what he meant. "Remember I told you the only living relative I could trace back to Nut was a woman by the name of Queen who happens to be his auntie?" Josh cleared his throat which felt dry as he talked. "Anyhow, I know you told me not to do anything without first contacting you and trust me, I called you several times but I had to get the ball rolling. I mean we are talking life or death matters, correct?"

"Look, just get to the point cause right now I'm already having this gut feeling that you're about to blow this whole fuckin' case with your Inspector Gadget strategies."

Joshua's entire facial expression changed to anger. "Well, for your information Magnum P.I., I'm sitting here with the only person who can bring Lester "nut" Jones to us. Say something Miss Queenie," Joshua ordered as he put the phone to Queen's ear. She was tied and bound.

"Whoeva in the fuck this is, go to hell! I hope Nut kill some mo' of you sick muthafuckas!" Joshua slapped Queen hard across the right side of her jaw with his left hand which was draped in a pair of brass knuckles.

"Josh, what the fuck is wrong with you? You stupid fuck! Don't you realize you're fucking up a top priority case? First, you're holding a potential witness against their will which in law terms is kidnapping, criminal confinement. In your case, it could be considered a terrorist hostage situation because, yes Mr. Skinhead, I did a little research on you and your college pranks ended up in our hate crimes profile. Not only that, it sounded like you just committed an assault. Please tell me you didn't put your hands on her you sick fuck!"

Joshua laughed out loud then burned the agent's ears with the next statement he made. "Well, well the way I see it is, either you're with me or against me and if you're against me you're the enemy and if you're the enemy…"

"Will you fucking shut the fuck up with the philosophy shit! Just tell me exactly where you are and let me take things from there." Agent Mondo knew he had to apprehend this lunatic before things got further out of hand. He'd done his own research and discovered Queen was an ex-con paroled to Atlanta,

Georgia. He prayed Joshua did not take his psychotic ass to Georgia.

"Now you know, that I know, that we know, that if I tell you my location you'd have hundreds of federal agents sniffing around my ass. So we're going to do this my way or no way. As much as I'd like to barbeque this nigger and feed her to a pack of hungry mountain lions, I know it would be worthless, especially since I have a taste for two people and two people only: Lewis and Nut. Now if this fine young lady cooperates and hand her nephew to me, hey, she lives to suck another pussy. But if she opens her mouth and disrespects me again, I will cut her body up into puzzle shaped pieces and send each piece to a police precinct in every state in America, including Puerto Rico. Now what I want is your undivided attention you concentration camp Jewish piece of shit. I need you to use your federal high-tech equipment and do a GPS track on a specific phone number. And please don't be a dumb fuck like your predecessor and try to trace my number. This phone was manufactured before GPS chips were put into phones. But understand this, Jewish boy, I'll be expecting call from you within the next 30 minutes with a 2-mile radius location on the number I'm about to give you."

Agent Taroski was already in the process of emailing the federal office in Atlanta, Georgia. He was more than 99.9% sure that Joshua was dumb enough to go directly to Queen's house. Once he got the number he would do his own investigation without this dumb fucker's approval. Joshua was just another pawn in the game of life that would be sacrificed for not playing the proper position. "Alright man, you got the upper hand. I just don't want no more innocent people getting hurt. Can you understand that? But, before you speak, just give me a lil more than 30 minutes and I'll be able to give you the exact location. I want this fucker just as bad as you. Hell, it's enough barbeque for all of us to eat." Mondo tried to sound as convincing as possible.

"Yeah, whatever you say you Jewish fuck." Then he rattled off the number to Mondo. "But I'm telling you, one screw-up and I'll fold this bitch up like a pretzel and shove her in her own oven. And another thing you scumbag, as long as I'm allowing you to breathe the same air I breathe, don't ever raise your voice and disrespect me!" The phone line went dead and that was the end of the conversation.

At that moment Agent Taroski received an email from the Atlanta Office just as he hung up the phone: *Agent Ty Daniels 404-555-6627 Call as soon as you disconnect from the bastard! We are in route to the address you gave us.* Mondo picked up his phone and dialed the number on the screen. Agent Daniels picked up on the first ring.

"We're two minutes from the suspected hostage location. Run this bastard's profile down to me once more."

Mondo smiled. "We're dealing with a known member of a white supremacist group known as The Supreme White Knights. They're an off-branch of the skinheads, a bunch of college wannabes trying to make a name. Anyhow, he's psychopathic, armed and a dangerous, delusional freak. There will be no negotiations. Shoot to kill. Take him down by any means necessary."

CHAPTER 9

"You know I'm really getting the urge to jump over this desk and beat the dog shit outta you! Is that what you want me to do? Must I proceed to SHOVE MY FOOT UP YOUR FUNKY BLACK ASS?" Captain Smith had just received a report from his superiors upstairs, confronting his department about sloppy investigations conducted by his detectives in homicide. There was one issue and one issue only: Who was in charge of the hospital massacre homicides? Captain Smith had the answer sitting in front of him. He was under a lot of stress and had a 5 o'clock news conference where he was going to explain to the public that his department fucked up.

"I know how things look, but sir you know just like me that my caseload is so heavy that sometimes even the smallest things can get overlooked. I mean, put yourself in my sh…" Sergeant Lewis was sweating and trying to explain himself. The tiny office reeked of sour cream and onion chips and since the A/C was not properly working the little desk fan only recycled funk. The Captain cut him off in mid-word, but what happened next caught him off guard.

"FUCK! And suddenly Captain Smith grabbed the desk fan and threw it at Lewis them jumped over the cluttered desk with his fist balled up. Documents, police reports and other papers went flying everywhere along with an old cup of coffee, a box of donuts and framed family photos. He grabbed Lewis by the neck and began to knee him in his pelvis, ribcage and he punched him in his left kidney.

Lewis couldn't control his built-up anger any longer. This time he fought back, throwing right and left hooks at the speed of lightning. He went into boxing mode and ducked several punches thrown by Captain Smith. Captain Smith came at Lewis with a lowered chin but Lewis lifted it up with a swift uppercut.

"Help! Help! Officer down! Get him off me! He's gone crazy!" Captain Smith yelled as he lay on the floor bleeding, trying to wrestle Lewis off him. As he struggled to reach for his ankle pistol the door came crashing in.

"What the hell?" a detective yelled as several others grabbed Sergeant Lewis off the top of Captain Smith.

"Cuff him and arrest him. He assaulted me. Restrain his ass!" the Captain ordered.

The other officers looked around lost, not knowing what to do. One of the rookies pulled his cuffs out and tried to force them on Lewis. He had a difficult time because Lewis attempted to put in a quick jab to his shoulder. Once this happened several other officers got involved and restrained Lewis. One had him in a chokehold and a full nelson while another officer held his legs to keep them from kicking wildly.

"Yeah, yeah get him boys. Put the cuffs on his fuckin' neck. Yeah, that's right. Captain Smith quickly walked over to Lewis to strike him but he slipped on several pieces of paper, lost his balance, knocking two officers down. Embarrassed and pissed off, he yanked one officer from the floor and stripped him of his Taser. He turned the voltage up and walked over to Lewis and shoved the Taser into his groin area and pulled the trigger. Sergeant Lewis began to scream and then to shake causing the officer that had him in a chokehold to let him go. As he fell to the floor Captain Smith reached for another's officer's nightstick. He struck Lewis several times in the midsection and then raised the five pound stick over his head to release the final blow.

CHAPTER 10

Sitting on Queen's couch, Joshua became very uneasy. He knew he couldn't trust Agent Mondo Taroski and now he realized he'd made a dumb-ass mistake in notifying an agent and putting everything he worked so hard for in jeopardy. Queen lay on the sofa across from Josh bound and hogtied. Her eyes were bloodshot red and she'd already pissed on herself twice. Josh thought about getting high and forcing her to get high but changed his mind. This was all business and no play. He had given Taroski long enough to return his call and now it was time to take things into his own hands. His mind was made up. He was going to torture Queen until she gave up everything he wanted to know. He stood up and stretched and began to taunt her.

"Oh well, I guess no one's coming to your rescue. I was just starting to like you; oh well." He walked over to the curtains just to take a quick glance out at his surroundings. As soon as he opened the thin white curtains he never saw what was coming.

The only thing Queen saw was the back of his head explode while his body was blasted into mid-air, jerking before he fell to the floor. As she looked up in shock she realized the front window was completely shattered and glass, blood and brains were everywhere. She began to scream but her cries were muffled by the duct tape covering her mouth. She tried to wriggle herself off the couch, but with her arms and legs bound it was very difficult. Using all her strength, she managed to get off the couch and stand so she could hop to the door, trying to avoid all the glass. As she hopped towards the door, she paused and glanced to the right at the madman who had held her captive for the last several hours. Then suddenly, the front door exploded off its hinges.

"Get the fuck down! Get down!" someone yelled at her.

Queen was frantically shaking her head back and forth, trying to talk through the duct tape. She was trying to tell the SWAT team the maniac was dead but they shouted for her to put her hands in the air. Queen rolled her eyes. Now I know they see all this tape around me and shit she said to herself. When she didn't comply one of the men rushed her and lifted her off her feet.

Agent Ty Daniels rushed in screaming, "Put her down! She's the victim!"

The young officer who tackled her felt stupid not realizing she wasn't a threat because she was all tied and bound up. As he stood up he saw blood was on his left hand. He checked himself for any open wounds then looked down at Queen whose arms were still tied behind her back. A shard of glass was sticking into her right wrist from where the young agent had tackled her to the floor before he swooped her up. He carefully pulled the tape off her mouth and got an earful of profanity.

"You dumb muthafucka, help me! Argghh! I can't believe you goof troops!" Her wrist was bleeding badly but the ties around her wrist kept pressure on it and somewhat stemmed the blood flow.

Agent Daniels knelt down beside her and said, "Let's get these things off your wrists." Then Queen blacked out.

CHAPTER 11

Diamond had just returned home from a long day downtown trying to speak in Star's defense. After finally convincing the judge and the DA that Star was the victim, Star was released into the custody of Fulton County Child Protective Services and placed in a group home. When Diamond turned onto her block she was surprised to see her street filled with spectators, news reporters and it looked like the entire police force. She knew something very serious must have happened because there was crime tape everywhere. She tried to drive through the crowd but the police stopped her. She got out of the car and pulled out her I.D., showing the two cops she lived at the house in question, and they let her run underneath the crime tape toward the house. She saw two stretchers being wheeled out the house and down the walkway. One occupant was completely covered up and the second occupant was attached to a machine and hooked up to I.V. bags and other unidentifiable objects. "Please Lord, don't let Queen be on one of those stretchers," Diamond prayed silently.

As she ran over toward the stretchers several officers held her back. "This is my fuckin' house! What the fuck is going on?" She looked over at the stretcher moving past her and saw Queen's tattooed arm. "Oh my God! she exclaimed as she ran over to the stretcher and looked down at Queen who had an oxygen mask over her face.

"Ma'am, she's going to be fine. Please back away so we can get her to the hospital. You can ride in the ambulance if you like but we must hurry. It's your decision," the paramedic said as they lifted Queen's stretcher into the back of the ambulance and secured it.

"I'm going with y'all." Diamond started to get into the ambulance when she felt a tight grip on her arm.

"No, you're coming with us. We have some questions to ask you. Let's start with a real easy one — where's Lester Jones aka Nut?" Agent Daniels asked as he placed cuffs on Diamond's wrist.

* * * * * * * * *

As Captain Smith prepared to deliver the final blow, he was stopped by one of his fellow officers. "Yo'! He ain't worth it Cap, he ain't worth it. You just need some fresh air."

Smith dropped the nightstick and looked at Lewis with fury and fire in his eyes. "You're finished, buddy. Do you hear me? Your ass is barbeque. I want your badge and pistol on my desk by the time I return!" Lewis just rolled around on the floor, gripping himself from pure pain. Smith knew he just couldn't fire Lewis but he could definitely suspend him until further notice. He walked out the office and headed toward the elevator. "What the fuck y'all looking at? Get back to work and I mean right now!"

Every plainclothes detective went back to their regular duties while rolling their eyes. Captain Smith watched them "hop to it" as everyone turned back to their iPods, laptops and whatever else they'd been doing. He felt a sense of power as he got on the elevator. The department was still in his hands and he would now have to make an example out of Lewis. He would run the department with an iron fist and zero tolerance. As Captain Smith stepped off the elevator and walked past the City Clerk's office, he told himself without a doubt, he would attend church this week. He walked outside and took in a lung full of fresh air. Then he got angry all over again at what he saw. He'd made it his personal duty to keep the taxi cabs from parking in front of City Hall. It seemed as if the foreigners didn't understand simple instructions, especially the African or the Arab cab drivers. The Caucasian Yellow Cab drivers always followed the law of the streets and stayed in line. As the Captain walked with a "tuff guy" strut towards the cab, he already had it in his mind that he was going to tow this piece of shit vehicle and set these "towel heads" straight once and for all. He walked up to the driver's side window and knocked loudly while yelling, "Step out the fuckin' car right now!"

The young looking African brother, dressed in a loudly colored tropical butterfly patterned shirt, continued to puff on his cigarette while rolling down the window. "Hey, hey calm down mister. Me was justa pullin' off in me car. Please accept my deepest apologies."

The strong African accent made it clear to Smith that maybe he was just as dumb as he looked and didn't know any better. "Look Kunta Kinte, I don't give two fucks about your broken English, your poor-ass country or if you are even a legal immigrant. But next time this piece of shit is parked anywhere in front of my jail, I'm hauling your ass in." The Captain turned and started to walk away thinking to himself there's no need to walk to his car and waste gas to go get lunch when he could have this dumb fuck take him around the corner. The cab was about to pull off when he reached out and opened the back door and got in and sat down. Then he thought maybe he should have driven his own car. Oh what the hell. He tapped on the glass divider that separated the driver from the passenger to get the guy's attention.

"Where to, my friend," the African asked.

"Oh, pull in front of the Subway just up the street."

The cab driver thought to himself that the drive wasn't even a half block away. Then he said, "Lazy fuck," out loud.

Captain Smith knew he heard him correctly but wanted to make sure he wasn't trippin'. "What the fuck you say?"

The African made eye contact with the Captain through his rearview mirror and smiled. "Oh no me friend, me say today's your luck." But as the cab pulled within five feet of the Subway restaurant, the driver accelerated to a speed of at least 60 miles per hour.

"Goddammit, hey, what the fuck is wrong with you?" The Captain began to pound on the glass aggressively. He could see the African laughing through his rearview mirror. The driver turned up the radio which was tuned to a hip-hop station. The music blasted through the speakers: "*Ready or not, here I come, you can't hide...I'm gonna find you...*" Lauryn Hill's (The Fugees) voice sounded like death to Captain Smith. He reached for the door and screamed in pain as he wrapped his fingers around a razor-laced door handle. He reached for his pistol and shouted, "Die motherfucker!" as he emptied the clip at the glass divider which he soon realized was bulletproof.

The driver turned down the radio. "Hey you back there, quiet down." Then he put in a cassette tape. "Maybe you'll enjoy this." What Smith heard made him shit on himself.

"Hello Captain, I mean Uncle Tom-ass nigga. By now you've probably pushed me to the point of being desperate. Don't worry though, we on the same team. Remember?"

The Captain listened as Smith's voice boom through the speakers, laughing. He began to pound on the backseat windows with no luck. He felt extremely hot and was breathing heavily.

The African, who was actually Nut, had turned the heat up in the back of the cab to the maximum. The tape continued to play.

"Now listen up, bitch cause right now you probably acting like the scary bitch you are, hiding behind the badge. I've put up with your shit for too long, pushing your rank around, talking to me like I was nothing more than your verbal punching bag. Now the tables are turning. My, my, my as you suspected, yeah I fucked over some reports; did a little dirty work here and there but all that's irrelevant Mr. Smith. Oh, by the way, my lil friend driving is gonna take real good care of you. Nut, say hello to Mr. Smith and Mr. Smith, say hello to Nut. I hope you two get real acquainted. Well, right now I'm probably clearing out my desk or who knows; I might be fucking your wife and daughter, but…gotta go."

"I'll kill you Lewis! I'll fuckin kill you!" Smith yelled. Then it dawned on him he was only yelling at a pair of 6x9 speakers.

Nut pulled the cab up to Laneka's house. He slid open a portion of the divider glass which was only large enough for a passenger to stick their hands through. "We can do this the easy way or the hard way. Slide both your hands through this window."

The Captain's heart began to beat wildly. He was in a no-win situation. He pushed both his wrists through the small opening and listened as the cuffs closed with a clink. Nut got out of the cab. He opened the back door of the cab and instructed Captain Smith to walk towards the back door of the house. Nut looked at the cab's back window which was splattered with so much blood it looked like a sick horror scene out of a Wes Craven movie.

Nut reached around the Captain and opened Laneka's back door with his .357 in his hand. His entire motive was to place the Captain at Laneka's house and make her death seem like a homicide/suicide crime scene. After doing his own research, he discovered Captain Smith was an undercover trick who couldn't keep his dick in his pants. With all the evidence Nut put into play, it would look like Laneka's boyfriend got out of prison so she wanted to cut everything off with Smith who just lost it. Nut was truly a mastermind. As he led Smith into the house he did a quick visual to make sure no one had been in the house since he left. "Sit yo' ass right here in this chair muthafucka and don't say shit."

Smith began to cry. "Youngsta, I don't know what Lewis done put you up to but please don't do this. You already kidnapped, assaulted and injured a Captain, don't make this shit worse. Lewis is a snake. He's just using you to get to me. I can help you young man."

Nut backhanded Smith. "Didn't I tell you to shut the fuck up? Let's get you out of these clothes." As Nut pulled off Smith's pants he felt a bulge in his pants pocket. He reached inside and pulled out Smith's wallet. Nut flipped through it quickly and threw it down. Then he took off Smith's shirt. When he looked on the kitchen floor at the open wallet he saw a Sam's card, platinum Visa card, a prepaid MasterCard and a police I.D. card. Then he noticed a photo that looked very familiar. While pointing the gun at Smith he took a few steps backward and picked up the photo. Nut couldn't believe his eyes. This must be one of his sick dreams he thought. "Where you get this fuckin' picture," he yelled.

At first Smith didn't realize Nut was talking to him. "Um, um what you mean?"

Nut became angry. "Don't fuckin' play with me. Where did you get this picture?" He walked over to Smith and pressed his pistol into his jaw while holding the photo in front of him.

"That's a picture of my daughter and her kids and my grandbabies. My daughter's no longer living."

Nut pulled back the hammer on the .357.

CHAPTER 12

"Now let's back it up just a little. You say this Nut character killed your ex-pimp years ago, correct?" Agent Daniels was satisfied with his interrogation skills. After convincing Diamond that no charges would be filed against her for the pistol they found in her house along with the ounce of marijuana in exchange for information on Nut.

Diamond felt like the weight of the world dropped off her shoulders. She just couldn't believe she was turning on her daughter's father. What Nut, Queen and no one else except Diamond knew was that Star was her and Nut's daughter. When Diamond moved to Atlanta she couldn't risk trying to raise a child and survive at the same time. So she turned Star over to the state and for the last 13 years she monitored her whereabouts and such. She and star became close and several times Diamond had to catch herself from telling her she was her mother. All that changed last night when Star cut up her foster mother's boyfriend's face. Diamond and Star talked for hours at the Waffle House before turning herself in.

"You gone get me back, mama?" was Star's last request.

"Yes baby," was Diamond's answer. Now she found herself turning on the only man whoever respected her and treated her like a woman.

"Okay ma'am, we're going to record your statement and have you sign some papers so we can get you out of here. But first, we've got to read you your rights."

Diamond shut her eyes briefly and opened them as she shook her head. "Nawl, I can't do this. Y'all manipulating me. I want to see my lawyer." The two agents looked at each other confused. "I know my rights and I want to see my lawyer. Fuck that gun charge and that punk-ass weed. I ain't helping you crackers solve shit, I ain't signing shit, I don't know shit, so eat shit!"

The lead agent slammed his fist onto the table. "You just made the worse mistake of your life, smart-ass!" He walked over to the door and yelled, "Let her get her free call and then take her to the coldest cell Fulton County has to offer."

* * * * * * * * *

As Diamond sat in a cell with seven other women whose charges ranged from prostitution to boosting, she thought about her life. She walked her 5'6", thickly built frame back and forth around her bunk area before sitting down again. She wanted to unbutton her jeans badly because she needed to relax and breathe but knew these unfamiliar faces would look at her as prey. She slipped off her pink and grey Air Max's and used them as a headrest so she could at least gain some comfort.

"Bitch, I know you hear me talking to you. Whore, what size shoes are those?"

Diamond thought she had dozed off but when she looked up there was a dark-skinned, heavyset woman standing over her. She stood at 6'2" and weighed every bit of 285 pounds of fat. The woman was tying her micro-braids up in a scarf as she confronted Diamond.

"Betsy, I think she ignoring you," one of the other women yelled out.

"Yeah, I think she figure she too good to talk to us," a crack addict threw in, trying to instigate.

"Bitch, the shoes, right now!"

Diamond was by far not a punk but she didn't want to put herself in a position to have to fight all these women. "Look, I ain't fuckin' with you, am I? No, I'm just sitting here minding my own business. But it's always one tuff bitch who wanna…" The woman slapped Diamond across the face before she could finish her last remark. The slap caught Diamond by surprise but now she was boiling with anger.

"Yeah bitch, Agent Daniels told me to rough yo' lil sassy ass up and that's what I'm 'bout to do."

After years of taking beat downs from Sam, her ex-pimp, Diamond had enrolled in some self-defense classes when she got to Atlanta. These classes were also helpful against unruly teenagers who hung around the Boys and Girls Club causing problems. Diamond's instincts kicked in and she held up her guard when the woman rushed towards her wildly. Diamond kicked her in the stomach area, causing her to lose her balance. The woman tried to grab ahold of Diamond to keep from falling but Diamond sidestepped her, leaving nothing but air for the woman to grab onto. With no balance and nothing to stop her huge body from falling, she fell headfirst into the stainless steel toilet, instantly cracking her skull open from the impact of her head hitting the metal and killing her. Blood flowed from her head as if the toilet was flushing.

"Oh my God!" one of the women screamed. "This crazy bitch done killed Betsy! Deputy, help us!" she screamed from the cell. All the women began crowding around the bars and yelling for help.

Diamond just looked down at the tragic scene. She shook her head back and forth. She couldn't believe what just happened.

She hadn't even touched the woman except for the kick. "Damn, I done fucked up," she whispered to herself.

The cell doors rolled open and several guards rushed in, spraying mace while pushing inmates out of the way. "Get down! Put your face down on the ground, now!" They cuffed Diamond and lifted her up from the floor and carried her out of the cell. Betsy would be pronounced dead at the scene. The women reported that Diamond tried to bully them. Diamond charges changed from possession of a firearm and marijuana to a murder charge.

CHAPTER 13

I don't know if this is God's way of telling me I need to change. I really don't care. At this point in my life I've lost everyone and everything that mattered to me. I never asked to be brought into this cold world. Anybody I knocked down deserved to be killed from Desmond, Julio, C-Dollas, them punk-ass security guards and so on. Growing up I had morals. The nightlife was never for me; the partying, pills, coke, liquor, multiple women, gangbanging and things of that nature never turned me on. Bringing pain to those who didn't know what pain felt like is what made me smile. Accepting a job and doing it right was what got my rocks off.

I could have sold kilograms of cocaine, but everybody ain't a drug dealer. I could of robbed plenty of niggas, but I'm not a stick-up kid. The lane I chose is the reason I know when I get to hell, me and Lucifer gone be beefing. Ke-Ke, damn girl, it's like once I lost you I just lost all hope. Everything I worked so hard for went down the drain. People might say I'm a lunatic, a psycho, even a basket case, but I'm just me. Now I got this old muthafucka tied up and if what he's saying is true, then he's my grandfather, huh? He's asking for mercy but what about when I needed mercy. Where was he at? I guess you have to change sometime in life. We can't keep walking down the same road, can we? Or should we?

While Nut was in deep thought his phone rang. He noticed the number and smiled. He hadn't spoken to his uncle in a few weeks since Ke-Ke's death. Although he really didn't want to answer the phone, he had to because his uncle would never call back-to-back. It had to be serious. Nut answered his phone, "Talk…"

CHAPTER 14

Welcome to Atlanta

Taz, as usual, was rushing frantically around her house trying to do her last minute packing before her 4:50 flight headed to Houston, Texas. This would usually be a trip with about 4 or 5 girls, but at the last minute she and her normal flock of friends fell out. Everything for the trip was booked in Taz's name and booked on her credit card, so she decided to go alone. She had always been a very outgoing woman and wasn't going to let the bickering of silly bitches stop her from hitting up Texas. At 26, Taz was a very well-shaped lady and had a beautiful caramel complexion and stood about 5'5". She had the body of one of those fine-ass strippers you find at the Onyx Club down in Atlanta, Georgia and was always wearing something that turned the heads of every straight man in Georgia.

Her favorite event was the NBA All-Star Weekend. She had lost seven pounds and about two to three inches off her waist specifically for this event, not to mention the flight and hotel room was nonrefundable. "So I'm definitely not about to miss my trip," she mumbled to herself as she took the pin curls out of her shoulder length, cinnamon red hair, standing in front of the bathroom mirror. "Tired ass bitches, these hoes really on some dumb shit. How you gone not go out of town over some shit another bitch said about a nigga that ain't even yours, huh? Don't make me no difference; these bitches not gone trick me out of a good time. I'm outta here, baby." Once she finished putting on her concealer, mascara and sprayed herself with her Daisy perfume by Marc Jacobs, she grabbed her two Heys suitcases and jumped into her Beemer and headed for Hartsfield International Airport.

Taz was born May 7, 1991, the first child of three. As a kid she was very quiet and always on the edge. Life was devastating growing up as a 6-year old girl in a small one-bedroom apartment with a trifling mama and an abusive stepdad. She started growing up that Sunday morning in 1997 after church on Easter Sunday.

"Girl, go in that room and take that damn dress off. You know I ain't spending another dime on no damn dress you only wear once a year," her mama, Thelma, yelled as she sat in her room with her 53-year old so-called husband who was almost 30 years older than her. Toney was a prime example of an old-ass fuck nigga. He was an alcoholic, womanizer, abusive and worse of all a fucking crack-head. While at the bus stop one Thursday morning on the west side of Atlanta, Toney ran into Thelma while carrying a whining baby. Thelma was struggling and didn't even have enough money to catch the MARTA bus.

"Don't worry about it sweet thang, I got an extra MARTA card," Toney told her. Not deep into his drug habit at this point and time, Toney still had his looks and swag even though this child he was flirting with was young enough to be his daughter.

"Thank you, sir. I swear my child's father ain't shit. Sometimes I feel like I hate his ass." The truth was Thelma's baby's daddy was dead. He was shot in a shootout between some guys from Bowen Homes and Hollywood Courts, two notorious projects in Atlanta who'd had beef for years. She didn't have her bus fare because she went in on half a dime bag of weed the night before. After giving Thelma his number, Toney received a call the same day from her asking, "Can you help me?" That's all he needed to hear.

Toney was known for turning young women out with sex and a nasty introduction to cocaine. After moving in with Toney, Thelma seemed to think things were going cool at first. Once she received her Section 8 housing voucher they moved to Zone 3 Mechanicsville, dead in the heart of the trap. Toney became very abusive, controlling and possessive. Everything was "Bitch, where you think you going?" or "Bitch, take that little-ass skirt off" or "Bitch, I need your whole check this month." It was always bitch this and bitch that with Toney. Thelma was trapped early with Toney. Because of her cocaine habit and Toney's sex, she wasn't going anywhere. Eventually, things got worse. The cocaine no longer fulfilled Toney's "monkey" so he moved on down the ladder to "crack." With Thelma's check, Section 8 voucher and no bills, Toney was in smoker's heaven. After one blast of crack he was hooked. And after lacing Thelma's blunt one day with crack, so was she. At this point there was no hope, no point of return.

"Taz, if I tell yo' lil ass to get out of them clothes again I'ma beat the shit out of you," Thelma said as she put the glass dick into her mouth and took a full blast.

"Baby, you enjoy that hit while I check on her little fast ass," Toney told her as he left the room in his boxers. And catching Taz off-guard in the middle of taking off her dress, Toney couldn't help but admire the sight before him.

This was the day Taz's nightmares began.

* * * * * * * * *

"Because neither one of us, wants to be the first to say goodbye..." Veronica sang as she headed to her baby's daddy Dre's house. After finally getting approved for her business license and getting the okay from Georgia's Childcare Services to open up her new

daycare facility, she needed a long vacation. "Somewhere, anywhere just as long as it is outside of Georgia," Veronica told her cousin Shonte on the phone. "I'm just sick of seeing these same people, dealing with Dre's same bullshit and I need a break." She had chosen Houston because she'd heard their Galleria Mall was some good retail therapy; and with all she had been going through she needed that. She had taken her girls to Disney World the weekend before and this weekend she wanted some time alone. Of course, she didn't tell Dre she was going out of town. She knew that he would not keep the girls because he was a hating-ass nigga, and he would question where she was getting all this money to sponsor all these trips outside Atlanta. In addition, she had a Mercedes Benz she had been lying about, telling him it was a rental, and that would definitely set off a red flag in his head. She decided to lie and tell him she had a class to attend for the daycare center she was trying to open. She needed someone to watch the girls until Monday morning.

Veronica was 25 years old and a beautiful, dark-skinned girl from around-the-way. She had one of those athletic bodies like Venus Williams. She wasn't as thick but you could tell she worked out. She was toned without an ounce fat on her body. She had pretty pearly white teeth with long jet-black hair that was always shiny and natural looking. She was definitely a beautiful, quiet girl who had never really had a chance to experience life. With her newfound fortune from her mother's life insurance policy, she was finally about to see the world. Later, after leaving her daughters with their father, she headed to the airport, blasting Maxwell, to start off a peaceful weekend with no one but her, her credit cards and a plush hotel room at Houston's Hotel Derek.

* * * * * * * * *

"*Mommy, wakeup, please mommy, stop playing and wakeup,*" *Veronica said to her mama, Vita, as she looked at the syringe that lay deep in a vein in her mama's left arm which was jerking up and down. Veronica remembered what her mama told her, "If I'm asleep and don't wake up, loosen the belt around my arm and put a cold rag on my head. Then slowly pull the needle out of my arm."*

Veronica had curiously asked her mama, "Mommy, why does your medicine always make you sleep and wake up at the same time when my medicine just puts me to sleep?"

Vita just smiled. "Chile you ask so many questions. You should be a prosecutor when you get older."

Veronica scrunched up her face in thought. "What's a prosecutor?"

Vita had laughed but this time it was no laughing matter. Vita would not wake up. Veronica did not want to call her daddy because every time her mama took her medicine her daddy threatened to take Veronica away for good. Veronica ran from the bathroom into the trash-littered kitchen and grabbed her teddy-bear, Poopie. She went into her room and hugged him until she went to sleep herself. Then she was awakened by a loud sound, BANG, BANG! "Vita, open this goddamned door! Veronica! Vita!" BANG, BANG! BANG! Still half asleep Veronica would recognize that voice from anywhere. It was her father, Paco.

She walked through the small living room which was filled with cheap Value City furniture that smelled of bacon and stale cigarettes and opened the door for her daddy, her superman. Paco, who stood 6'6" and resembled Denzel Washington, aggressively stormed in. "Hey pudding pie, where yo' mama at? "Vita! Vita!" he called out. "And look at this goddamn house…" she heard as he walked towards her mama's room. But when he got near the bathroom he yelled, "Vita!!" Before Veronica could say anything her father rushed into the bathroom shouting, "God no, no, no, baby! Dammit woman, look what you done did!" He hurried up and shut the bathroom door and locked it. Being an ex-paramedic he tried to revive Vita after checking her pulse, which was dead. He administered CPR but to no avail—she was gone. After crying and sobbing for what seemed like hours to him he heard a small fist knocking on the door.

"Daddy, open the door. I gotta pee real, real bad. Mama, tell daddy to open the door."

"Baby, go down the hall to Mrs. Rosa's apartment right now until I come down there."

Veronica became impatient. "But why daddy? I gotta pee!"

Paco became furious in his grief. "Girl, do what the hell I said!"

Veronica raced out the apartment. Paco had never laid hands on her but when he raised his voice he sounded like God."

After taking the syringe, belt and spoon with dope residue and disposing of them, Paco picked up Vita and carried her into her bedroom and laid her on the bed. Then he shut the door and walked down to Mrs. Rosa's apartment to use her phone to call an ambulance because Vita's phone always stayed disconnected. He had prayed day in and day out that God would deliver Veronica to him and away from Vita, but not like this.

After explaining to Veronica that she was coming home with him all she kept asking was, "Is mama still sleep? Dang, when she gone wake up. I hate her medicine."

Paco looked at his precious daughter with tears in his eyes and replied, "Yeah, I hate her medicine, too, kiddo. Unfortunately things were not as easy as they seemed. Paco couldn't get full custody of Veronica because of his past. He had been arrested for murder, kidnapping and robbery five years ago and went to trial and won due to lack of evidence and police tampering. Since the victim was a retired state trooper the case was high profile and every courtroom in Georgia knew the name of Paco Paris. When he arrived at child custody court in Dekalb County, not only did Vita's family "throw salt" on him but they hired an attorney to bring up his past.

"The court finds that even though all charges were dropped on you Mr. Paris, you're a menace to society. I would never destroy this child's life by turning her over to a savage like you; a cop killer," said the judge. Paco tried to explain that it was a case of mistaken identity— which was actually true—but the judge banged his gavel and said, "One more outburst cop killer and I'll have you thrown in prison for terroristic threats on a judge."

Paco gritted his teeth after watching Vita's sister smile, point and laugh at him. They didn't want Veronica either. They just wanted her insurance money she would collect for the death of her mother. Paco had convinced Vita to let him pay for life insurance because her way of life was not healthy. But she didn't care as long as it wasn't coming out of her pockets. That was why Paco removed all the drugs and evidence from the scene. He knew that some insurance companies ruled overdosing as suicide which would mean no money for Veronica.

After the toxicology report came back from the autopsy it wasn't raw heroin that killed Vita, it was a "hot shot"—slang in the street for rat poison—so her death was ruled a homicide; and of course the police tried to pin it on Paco Paris but couldn't. Veronica was to collect $550,000 from the insurance policy and the wolves were hungry. Paco had a feeling something like this would take place if Vita ever died so he made sure there was a clause in the policy. The policy mandated that Veronica would not have access to her money until she was 18 and could not cash out the money until her 25th birthday. Paco, who was educated himself, had been smart about Veronica's policy. He knew this was the only way to keep Vita's lowdown, money-hungry family out of Veronica's pockets.

After the judge explained the clause in the policy to Veronica's family, they were no longer interested in caring for her. What happened next changed Veronica's life. The judge banged his gavel continuously and shouted, "Order in the court! Order in the court! I hereby declare this child a ward of the state and due to negligence on both sides of the family, I am turning little Veronica Paris over to Child Protective Services caseworker, Pam Johnson, who has recommended a foster home for this child until she is legally an adult. I will review this case every 180 days and will remain open to all suggestions from family members; not a cop killer. Court is adjourned!"

Paco silently screamed as tears rolled down his face. But in the end he knew that once his baby girl turned 25, she would be set for life. This was a bittersweet moment.

* * * * * * * * *

A frustrated and angry Lola was stuck in traffic as she was leaving Lenox Mall. She screamed out the window of her Range Rover, "Damn bitch, move, with your raggedy-ass car! Don't you see me trying to get over?" As she merged off the exit her phone rings through her navigation system. "Yeah," she answers.

On the other end was her girlfriend Kim. "How far away are you from my house?"

"I'm pulling onto 14th Street now so I'm about three minutes away." Kim proceeds to tell her she is not home and is stuck in traffic 15 minutes away. Lola snaps, "Look bitch, you got 15 minutes to get there and if you're not there I'm leaving. I'm not about to miss my flight fucking around with you." Then she hangs up on Kim. Lola was 24 and a very pretty light-skinned girl. She was definitely model material. She always turned the heads of all the Atlanta elite including ball players, doctors, lawyers and especially young drug dealers. Lola was one of those type of girls who believed that money talks. If you had no coins you had no Lola. That's just who she was. Lola arrived and Kim wasn't there. After waiting around for about 22 minutes, Kim still hadn't arrived. Lola politely pulled her Range Rover out of the driveway and headed back to the expressway. She called Kim and said, "Bitch, the flight leaves in 72 minutes. If you not at the airport, I guess I'll just have to bring you back a baller." Then she hangs up on her and made her way to Hartsfield International Airport.

* * * * * * * * *

"But daddy, I want the pink Barbie car not the white one. Lola was what black folks called a bad-ass spoiled brat. She was one of those kids you would see showing out in the store and you would vow to beat the shit out of your kids if they ever acted like that.

"Honey, this is all they have left. Remember, it is Christmas."

Lola looked up at her father who was white and reminded her of Clint Eastwood said, "Soooo what! I'm not ever going to drive it then!" Lola stormed down the aisle of Toys R Us and left her father shaking his head.

"Lola, come back here Ms. Lady."

Lola stopped and turned around with her pig tails flying, folded her arms across her chest and poked out her lip. "What!!" she screamed.

Her father, Lonis, was soft. He was a pre-law student at the University of Georgia (UGA) and was determined to one day pass the bar and become a partner in a big firm. He never raised his voice, hit Lola or argued with her. Lola got what Lola wanted. Her mother, Sara, was a beautiful brown-skinned woman who had long hair and high cheekbones. She was also attending UGA to study computer science. Both of her parents came from wealthy backgrounds. However, Lonis' family was prejudiced and his family told him straight up "I ain't providing for no niggers or half-breed jigaboo nigglet babies."

"But father…" Lonis tried to explain.

"But my redneck ass. This family's history was built on pure American soil, not Africa. I ain't having my son marry no nigger into this family's name. You will never be a partner at my firm, going about life, mixing it up with some nigger bitch."

Lonis couldn't argue with his dad. After graduating top of his class, he married Sara and his father disowned him. So Lonis packed his family up and moved to Lithonia, Georgia to start his new life. He gave Lola anything she wanted; never raised his voice and treated her like his angel. "One day you're going to be a princess," Lonis would tell Lola.

"No daddy, I'm going to be a model."

Lonis laughed. It was like Lola to always get in the last word. Sara was a great wife and mother and was dedicated to her family. But it all changed on New Year's night in 1998. While driving back from Athens, Georgia after celebrating the holiday with Sara's family, Lonis' car was forced off the road by a large truck bearing rebel flags on the windshield. The car swerved off the road and into a ditch and all you could hear was Sara and Lola, crying and screaming. "Are you guys okay?" Lonis shouted. "What the hell was that guy thinking?" He unbuckled his seatbelt and twisted around to comfort Lola. Then he heard a loud banging on the driver's side window and when he turned his head to see what the noise was, he saw the face of his Uncle Terry, a dedicated Klansman. But it was too late. The heavy-set white man unloaded three shots from his shotgun into Lonis' car. BOOM! click-clack BOOM! click-clack BOOM! Then he left just as suddenly as he appeared. Two shots shattered Lonis' face and one ripped through Sara's arm. Lonis died instantly, covering Lola with blood as she sobbed and cried.

Sara was in total shock after seeing Lonis' face but thought about Lola and managed to crawl from the car and out the ditch where she flagged down several cars and the people assisted her in getting help. She, Lonis and Lola were rushed to the hospital via emergency helicopter. Sara was in a daze and told the police what happened but they changed her story and said it was a carjacking. The small racist community already felt that Lonis was a traitor. The truth was that his own father had him killed. When Sara told them a white man did it, the police had her sedated and put in a mental hospital where she is still being held. The police said her story was too unbelievable so she had to be traumatized.

Lola was taken in by Sara's family who were forced to move out of Athens after the death of Lonis. They relocated to Marietta, Georgia where Lola would grow up. Although Lola went through such a life-changing event at a very early age, she still managed to get through life pretty well. Lola was a very beautiful girl so her looks took her a very long way. Being that her dad had been a lawyer, Lola learned how to finesse her way by running game. Lola knew how to tell you exactly what you wanted to hear while making it sound truthful. She had skills. This would become Lola's new way of life; tricking men into giving her whatever she wanted based on her spoiled ways and good looks — just like she used to do daddy.

CHAPTER 15

Taz was about to work up a sweat as she stormed through the airport parking terminal. She didn't think there would be so much traffic on the expressway and she still had bags to check. She finally reached baggage check-in and then made her way to the security line. As she stood in line so many thoughts ran through her head. She wondered if she was going to score big this trip or if this weekend was going to be a waste of money. She wasn't worried that she was traveling alone because that's how bosses rolled. She knew that since she was alone she would probably have even more fun because that meant she didn't have to compromise what she wanted to do or answer to anyone.

She finally made it through security and got to the gate only to find out the flight hadn't even started boarding yet. It was actually delayed thirty-two minutes. She found an empty seat in the waiting area and pulled out her iPod to listen to Cardi B's "I Like it Like That." She was preparing mentally for the atmosphere in one of her most favorite places, Houston, Texas.

"Should anyone wish to upgrade their seat to first-class, you may come to the ticket counter and do so now," announced the gate agent.

Taz noticed a pretty dark-skinned girl make her way to the ticket counter. She concluded the girl must definitely work out because her body was the truth. She was debating if she should upgrade her seat as well but decides against it. So she settles back and listens to Cardi B on her iPod.

At the ticket counter Veronica was telling the ticket agent, "Yes, I'd like to upgrade to a first-class seat. She had never flown first-class before so she decided this was her perfect opportunity. As she headed back to her seat in the waiting room she noticed it had been taken by a mother with two kids. She could see, and hear, these kids were bad as hell. Knowing how it was traveling with kids, she didn't think twice about finding another seat. But as bad as those kids were, that mother was probably already stressed enough. She looked around and spotted a cute caramel skin-toned girl with cinnamon colored hair sitting alone on a bench. "Guess I'll sit by that bitch," she mumbled to herself. So she walked over to the bench, looked the girl up and down and then sat down. Then she tapped the girl on her shoulder.

Taz turned around and noticed the dark-skinned chick trying to get her attention. "Hi," Taz said.

"Hi," replied Veronica. "I just wanted to let you know I love your hair color. It matches your skin perfectly," Veronica said as she adjusted a heart-shaped locket around her neck.

"Thanks girl. I wanted to try something new for the festivities this week. You never know who you might run into," Taz said with a sneaky smirk on her face.

"Is Houston your final destination?" Veronica asked.

"Yes," Taz replied.

"You mentioned festivities, what festivities?" asked Veronica curiously.

Taz looked at Veronica as if she had lost her damn mind. "What do you mean 'what festivities'? Is Houston your final destination?" she asked Veronica sarcastically.

"Yes," said Veronica.

"Ummm okaaay, it's the NBA All-Star weekend and you didn't know that?"

"Ahhh, no," Veronica replied.

"Well, looks like you picked the perfect weekend and the perfect city to travel to this weekend. Girl, it's going down! Are you traveling alone?" Taz asked. But before Veronica can respond, Taz goes on to tell her how her trip was supposed to be with three other girls but they fell out of the plans. "So girl, I'm gone be down there by my damn self. I was supposed to be with my girls Myah and Angelica but them bitches be on some dumb shit. I wasn't gonna come but I told myself 'fuck these bitches!' I spent my money and I'm about to enjoy my weekend so here I am."

"Damn, you got to be kidding me. I can't believe I'm about to be at the NBA All-Star weekend. Girl, I have never been to an All-Star weekend. I just wanted to go to Houston to do some shopping; spend a little change. I didn't know it was going down this weekend. Girl, I'm empty-handed. I didn't bring nothing but my toothbrush and some panties. I'm going shopping when I get there," Veronica said excitedly.

As boarding began the girls exchanged numbers and made plans to do breakfast the next morning since both of them would be in town alone. Veronica proceeded to her first-class seat and Taz headed back to the coach section. They were both kind of elated that they'd found someone to kick-it with for the weekend. Veronica was especially excited that she was going to be in the midst of the NBA All-Star action and at one of hottest hotels in Houston. What neither girl realized was this was about to be a weekend that would change their lives and start a very close relationship...for better or worse.

CHAPTER 16

After a smooth flight to Houston—with no turbulence, a few Baileys and coffee—Taz reached into the overhead bin and grabbed her Burberry carryon and jockeyed into line to leave the aircraft. The flight was packed and it didn't help that an overweight Caucasian male rudely pushed past, smelling like he had shit on himself. "Funky-ass cracker," she said. He holding that laptop like somebody gone steal it when he need to be holding some air freshener next to his ass, she thought as she exited the plane. The airport was filled with different types of people. You had the young fly guys, the hood rats and even the pretty girls who acted like they've never been less than dimes their entire life.

As she stood in baggage claim, Taz noticed a handsome, bright-skinned guy standing next to her and giving her a reckless eyeballing stare. He was tatted up like a model straight out of Prison.com and he kind of favored Soulja Boy. She hated people staring at her so she politely asked him, "Can I help you?"

He looked her up and down, smiled, showing a mouth full of tacky gold teeth and replied, "Yeah, you can help me. Let's exchange numbers. I wouldn't want you to miss out on your blessing," he replied while pulling a cheap touchscreen TracFone from a Gucci case.

Taz rolled her neck and responded rudely, "Blessing, huh? Nigga, I didn't sneeze so I damn sure don't need you to bless me." She looked him up and down, rolled her eyes and walked away. She could hear his lame-ass homeboys laughing in the background and that added more fuel to her fire. She turned and walked over to the shortest one who stood a little over 5'11" and resembled a fake T.I. He was rocking a pair of Balmain jeans that she knew were knockoffs and a pair of Gucci sneakers that she had bought for her ex a few years back. Now she had ammo. She stopped in her tracks and turned to the Soulja Boy lookalike. "If you gone bless anybody, nigga, you can bless your man here with a pair of Gucci sneakers that are in season because them muthafuckas is not in this year's catalog and damn sure not in last year's if you want to get technical."

The short, brown-skinned man she was referring to took it personal. "Bitch, you got me fucked up, shawty. I got bands on deck," he yelled as he fumbled through his pockets trying to pull out his small $500 bankroll.

"Huh, listen lil T.I., get your grand hustle up and see if 100 grand can fit in them fake-ass Balmain pants," Taz said as she walked away, having wasted 10 minutes with those losers. The nerve of some men, she thought to herself. Niggas will do anything for some attention. Taz was not the one to let anyone have the last word either so she turned around and yelled, "Oh yeah, tell your bitch to give you her tax refund so you can get your hustle on!" She could tear your ass up with words. Everybody who knew Taz pretty much knew not to go there with her unless you wanted your feelings hurt. Then she heard a voice to her right.

"That nigga better be glad it wasn't me. I would have thrown a stack of money on his bitch-ass and told him to bless that."

Taz looked over and saw a very petite, light-skinned girl with short hair standing there. This girl was bad. She had the latest Luis Vuitton Courtney bag—the big one—with matching sandals. She was rocking a pair of stone-washed Seven Jeans with a revealing Victoria Secrets tank top. To finish it off she was wearing some of the biggest diamond earrings Taz had ever seen on a female other than Nicki Minaj or Cardi B. They looked like huge pebbles and reminded her of the ones R. Kelly wore on his TP2 album cover. This girl had beautiful skin with a nice set of teeth. She definitely had a Colgate smile. Taz knew that this woman was either in Houston meeting her NBA baller boyfriend, or was there to make some money some sort of way. Taz was a boss and could sniff out your resume quickly and right off the top she could already tell this woman wasn't the independent type at all. She looked to be about 24 and there was no way a woman that age could walk around the airport in over five thousand dollars' worth of clothing without performing some extra-curricular activities.

Taz replied, "Girl, okay, some niggas have the worst pickup lines."

Lola laughed and introduced herself. "I'm Lola, nice to meet you. I really can't believe the nigga tried you like that. Girl, I sat across from him on the flight and I thought he was a cutie. I guess some dudes just don't need to open their mouths."

Taz nodded her head in agreement. As the luggage belt began to circle around, Taz saw her Heys luggage coming around so she grabbed the handle and pulled it off the belt.

"Heys," said Lola. "Okay baby girl, looks like you have good taste."

Taz laughed and replied, "No, that's you Ms. Louis Courtney."

Both girls laughed and went their separate ways. Taz looked around but did not see the girl she had met at the airport earlier. She probably missed her in the midst of all that drama. Then again, Veronica had flown first-class which meant she would have gotten off the plane before Taz. Plus, Veronica had mentioned she came empty-handed and planned on shopping so she probably didn't have to wait on any luggage. She was probably already at her hotel. Taz planned on telling Veronica about the guy at the airport at breakfast the next morning. But what she didn't know was that today wouldn't be the last time she would run into that group of guys.

CHAPTER 17

As the day cooled down, Sergeant Lewis sat in the parking lot of the police station. He smiled as he watched the Yellow Cab drive off. The cab held hostage his only problem. He told himself that maybe it wouldn't hurt to get a quick 8-ball and call up Cherry again. Her stank ass was probably headed to Houston to strip and trick for the All-Star weekend. Fuck that ho! Sergeant Lewis had convinced himself he didn't need her. After the most recent incident with Captain Smith, Sergeant was happy to put this behind him. As he pressed his foot on the gas and attempted to drive off, his unmarked squad car was suddenly surrounded by other unmarked cars. "What the fuck?" he said out loud. Then several federal agents jumped out of their vehicles with weapons drawn, ordering Sergeant Lewis to exit his vehicle. Lewis held his badge out the window and yelled, "I'm a police officer, dumb-asses!"

Then a Caucasian male who looked like the swimmer, Michael Phelps, walked towards Sergeant Lewis' vehicle while signaling to the other federal agents to lower their pistols. "Lewis, Lewis, Lewis," said Agent Mondo Taroski sarcastically. "We've never met. But here's the deal. You're going to throw your keys out of the window. Once you are cuffed and read your rights, you will tell me where I can find Mr. Lester "Nut" Jones."

Sergeant Lewis was wondering who was this sucka but knew he was not in any position to try for a stalemate. He revved his engine but the federal agents drew their weapons again and moved in closer.

"Lewis, it's over. It's not worth it!" Agent Taroski yelled as he pulled and pointed his 40 Glock at Sergeant Lewis' face.

"Fuck! Goddammit!" Lewis began to sweat. But he turned off the car, threw his keys out the window and allowed himself to be arrested.

* * * * * * * * *

"I'm telling you this; Nut is one sick young man. He has threatened to force my wife into prostitution for money; he has even threatened to kill my wife; he has said he would kill me and several of my partners, including my mentor and best friend, Captain Smith. Lawd, he's a madman." Sergeant Lewis was a true coward and would rollover on his own mother if he knew he would gain from it.

"Lewis, I'm not buying anything you're saying right now. You've been under federal investigation for years. Now look at you, placing all your dirt on a low-life street punk." Taroski had become irritated with Lewis and wanted him in a cold cell by midnight.

"Look, I...I got proof. I can prove that all this is Nut. Lester Jones, he kidnapped the Captain and said unless my wife brought him three thousand dollars the Captain would die. I know exactly where they are. He's the animal. He has mules, eyes and ears in the department. He threatened to kill my wife!!"

Taroski decided to take Lewis up on the information he'd just heard. "So you're going to take me to this location, correct?" he asked.

"Yes, right now," stated Lewis.

CHAPTER 18

Taz got into her taxi and told the driver she was staying at the Hotel Derek. She had been to Houston before but couldn't really remember much about the city. The last time she was here was for a Super Bowl a few years back. One thing for sure, she definitely had to go back to Jack in the Box. They didn't have the franchise in Atlanta and she loved their egg rolls and milkshakes. On her way to the hotel Taz saw all kinds of whips in the city. It was early Thursday morning and the city was already flooded with ballers. She arrived to the hotel within 15 minutes. Before getting out the cab she texted her mother as well as Angelica and Myah— who still weren't talking to one another—to let everyone know she made it safely to the hotel.

As Taz was getting out the cab she saw Veronica getting out of a black Escalade. She must have gotten a rental car because she specifically remembered her saying she knew no one in Houston. She thought it was such a coincidence that she and Veronica were staying in the same hotel. She didn't suspect anything but Taz was a very cautious chick. They were two girls from the same city, on the same flight, staying in the exact same hotel. What were the odds of that? She dialed the number Veronica had given her.

"Hey Taz, what's up?" Veronica answered.

"Don't hurt nobody in that Big Boy Cadillac," Taz teased.

"Where you at, girl?" Veronica asked.

"About to check in at the Hotel Derek. Which one of my ex's sent you to stalk me cause there is no way we just so happened to be staying at the same hotel," Taz said. Both girls laughed.

"I'm about to head over to the Galleria to shop. If you want to put your bags up and ride with me you can," offered Veronica.

"Okay, cool. Come in for a second and we'll drop my bags and then let's hit the mall," said Taz. So Veronica parked her car and met Taz in the lobby.

As both girls walked through the hotel lobby they could hear screaming and yelling. They looked around and noticed all these people looking crazy; some white, some black. They were mostly the NBA All-Star game spectators trying to get settled in the city before all the groupies and broke folks showed up. As they got closer to the front desk, Taz could see Lola "going off" on both the phone and at the front desk clerk.

"Look at that damn high-yellow bitch showing out in this nice-ass hotel," Veronica said.

Taz looked and said, "Girl, that's Lola."

"You know her?" Veronica replied.

"Kind of, but not really. We were at baggage claim together," Taz said. She strained to hear what Lola was saying on the phone.

"So nigga, you really got me all the way down here and didn't pay for my room? It's all good, boo because trust and believe me I'll see you out this weekend and when I do you better hope your wife ain't with you cause her and the NBA gone know about a whole lot of fuck-shit you been doing!"

At that point Taz saw the front desk clerk motion for security and heard the clerk tell her, "Ma'am, I have told you several times we do not accept cash for deposits at the Hotel Derek. The La Quinta Inn does and its right down the road."

"And I have told you several muthafucking times that I can't find my goddamned card. And bitch, do I look like a La Quinta

Inn type of bitch? You gone take this cash and you gone take this shit now!" Lola snapped.

At that point Taz saw security head over to Lola at the desk. She knew where this was about to head. She told Veronica she would be right back and made her way to the front desk. By this time everyone was looking at Lola. You could hear snickering, laughing, people calling her a groupie and broke and any other name they could think of.

Taz taps Lola on the shoulder and says, "Girl, you better shut the fuck up before they lock your ass up. Let me handle this." Then Taz told the agent, "Check-in for Tashawn Vasquez please."

The clerk told Taz, "Ma'am, I'm going to have to ask you to step to the end of the line. There are people before you and we work on a first come first served basis."

Taz leaned in close to the clerk and said very professionally, "Look bitch, I just saved you from getting your ass whooped and from having them flustered-ass cheeks turn any redder from you getting your ass cussed out, too. If you want this young lady out your face I suggest you check me in and give me my fucking room key or she's not the only one you're going to have to worry about beating your ass before the end of the day."

The clerk rolled her eyes and turned bright red and without hesitation said, "Absolutely Ms. Vasquez. I just need your credit card and a valid I.D."

Taz looked over at Lola and winked and said, "Okay Ms. Louis Courtney, looks like you'll be staying with me until you get yourself situated." The clerk handed Taz the room keycards and Lola, Taz and Veronica headed to Taz's room to put up Lola and Taz's bags.

CHAPTER 19

Taz inserted the keycard into the slot of her hotel suite door, a green light appeared and it opened. The girls walked into one of the Hotel Derek's plush suites on a high level floor. The room was decked out. It was a two-bedroom suite with a living room and kitchen. It had 32" plasma TV's and was stocked with the latest wines and liquors.

"Taz, are you expecting company? I thought you said you were going to be alone for the weekend?"

"Girl, I am. I got a suite because there were originally four of us but the others dropped out and I ended up having to keep it because the hotel is sold out for the weekend. So there was no other option to downgrade."

Lola was on the phone, furious with her sponsor. After she hung up with him she told Taz, "Girl, thank you for saving my ass at the check-in desk. How much is the room? I can give you half right now. I have the cash. I just couldn't find my credit card to put the room on it."

Taz rolled her neck and said, "Girl, it's all good. Just figure out your situation so I can know if I should expect you here for the entire weekend or not. I'm going to tell you upfront I don't like liars and I don't like thieves. Just don't steal from me and you're straight."

Lola looked at Taz with an attitude and said, "No offense, I mean your Heys luggage is cute and all but I don't foresee you having anything in that little luggage that I would want. And I'm not sure if you noticed but I'm a size four and you're like a size what, 12 to 14? So I very seriously doubt if there's anything worth, I mean, if there's anything that would interest me in your bag."

Taz looked back and Lola and said, "That was a cute little introduction, red bone, but don't get it twisted because you got on a little Louis. You ain't fucking with me baby girl, hands down. Oh, and for the record, I'm a 9 and not a 14…"

Veronica jumped in and broke up the cat fight. "I don't care what size either one of y'all heifers is. I'm 'bout to hit this mall. So how much more of this bickering we got before we can leave? Oh, and by the way Lola, I'm Veronica. It's nice to meet you."

"Yeah, I saw you on my flight. You were in first-class, right?" Lola responded.

"Yes girl and I must say I see why people pay that extra money to sit up there. Not only was it some cuties, but they treated me like a fucking queen." Then the two girls began talking.

Taz had gone to the bathroom and she walked out fly as hell. She had on a pair of Seven blue jeans with rips at the knee, a cheetah print blouse with lots of cleavage showing, a Chanel brand bag with matching sandals and sunglasses. Lola burst out laughing. "Something funny?" Taz asked Lola.

"No bitch, but I see you had to show me you was working with a little something in that suitcase after all, huh?" All the girls laughed at that and headed out to get the Escalade to go to the mall.

After they're in the car the radio started playing one of Taz's favorite songs. Taz asked Veronica if she could turn it up. Veronica nods her head and Taz hit the volume. The song playing was "Like Dat" by Webbie featuring Lil Boosie. Then Taz started singing aloud, *"Like Beyoncé, like Trina, like a big booty-ass black diva, like a stripper, up and down like flipper, bend over and let me see it from the back."*

Lola interrupted Taz from the backseat. "Girl, this must really be your jam. You can't tell its old by the way you gyrating on that seat. Didn't you just meet her at the airport? And you already showing out in this girl's truck."

Taz turned around and said, "Girl, I don't give a damn! This is who I am and I'm going to be myself regardless of who likes it or not. Plus, Veronica ain't no saint. This car smells just like loud, so trust me she got a little hood in her, too."

Veronica turned to Taz and said, "Ha-ha. Yep, I keep cush on deck. You want some?"

"No, I don't smoke. I stay high off life," Taz replied.

"What about you Lo?" asked Veronica.

"Uh unh," said Lola. "Give me some Patrón or some Chardonnay and I'm straight. I don't want nothing I got to inhale, swallow or put up my nose."

As the girls were about to pull up to a red light, Taz noticed a fine, brown-skinned brother driving an aqua Bentley in the right lane next to them. As both cars reached the light Taz intentionally rolled down her window to make sure the driver could see her looking good in her Chanel frames. She acted as if she didn't see the guy and continued to dance to the song on the radio. The guy started honking his horn repeatedly at their Escalade. Taz turned her head to look at the driver.

"Damn baby, where y'all headed," he asked.

"The Galleria," Taz told him.

"Shit, where y'all from," the gentleman asked.

"The ATL baby."

"Oh, okay so y'all some Georgia peaches, huh?"

"Yep."

Taz could hear the guy's homeboy in the back seat asking, "Damn, who is the chocolate queen driving?"

"Oh, that's Veronica," Taz jumped in and replied.

The homeboy said, "Damn, tell Veronica if we can accompany y'all to the mall, she can have whatever she likes. Just throw that shit in the bag, ma."

"Oh yeah?" Taz said.

The driver said, "Oh yeah, that's how we rocking. As a matter of fact, it's three of y'all and it's three of us. Shit, we headed to the mall, too. Everything on us."

Taz looked at Veronica, Veronica looked at Lola and Lola looked at Taz. Two of the three agreed to follow the Bentley to the Galleria.

CHAPTER 20

The girls could tell that Lola wasn't really in the mood to be bothered. She had this look of disgust on her face. You could tell whatever was going on with her and her baller was not a good situation. Before they got out of the car Lola was texting. Taz told her, "I know you're probably not the happiest person right now, but girl we're here in Houston, Texas. It's the All- Star weekend and the city is full of people who are here and ready to have a good time. We haven't been in the city two hours and we're already about to get a shopping spree that's paid for. Let it go. We will see your boo when we hit the city tonight and trust me, we will stunt on his ass." Lola just looked at Taz, rolled her eyes and continued texting. "You can do all that all you want," Taz said. "But when we get in this damn mall you better fix your face. All three of these dudes cute and look like they getting it. So if you don't mind, I would like for us to show a little appreciation."

Lola replied, "Girl, I'm used to this type of shit. My nigga is a 4-time All-Star and takes good care of me. These niggas ain't gotta buy me nothing."

"Okay," said Taz. "Well, ya nigga don't want you right now and these niggas is being nice so either you gone smile or when we get in this mall, bitch you can go your own way and buy your own shit and we can meet you back at the car when we're done. Either way, you not about to fuck up my lick." Taz mumbled under her breath, "Bitch ain't gone fuck up my trip. Shit, that's why I left them other hoes at home. Fuck that, these hoes got the game wrong." She looked over at Veronica who was smiling. "What the hell you laughing at?" Taz asked.

Veronica replied, "I can tell this is going to be one hell of a weekend."

"You damn right it is," Lola agreed. The girls got out of the truck and followed the gentlemen into the Galleria Mall.

The driver of the Bentley was named Darryl. He was a 6'4", 215 pound, tatted-up, caramel complexioned, Nelly-looking brother. When he first opened his mouth Taz was happy he didn't have a grill full of gold teeth. Not only had the last scrub she ran into have a grill that looked like it came straight from the Flea Market, but coming from the south she was used to seeing every male, and almost every female, with gold teeth. It was a huge turnoff. But Darryl had some pretty pearly white teeth and she knew by his nicely manicured hands that whatever he did, he was the boss and never lifts a finger. Taz could see he was really, really feeling her and so far the feeling was mutual. Every store they walked past or approached, he would ask her if she wanted to go in.

"Look ma, it's all good, I got you."

This brother had a lot of swag. From his New York snap back hat down to his Cargo pants and Louis Vuitton tennis shoes he was definitely on. Taz smiled and said, "I already know you run into a lot of gold diggers, but I'm far from that. But since you insist, I can't argue baby." So she went into a few stores such as Neiman Marcus, Topshop, Gucci and surely these guys were not playing when they said everything was on them. By the time Taz finished grabbing a variety of new apparel in the Gucci store, she headed towards Darryl who stood by the register on his brand new iPhone.

"Damn shawty, you done already? You down in Houston now and as Lil Flip told you, 'this is the way we ball.' So treat yourself, don't beat yourself."

Taz thought to herself either this nigga was rich, flipping bricks, spending counterfeit money, or got fake credit cards cause a bitch ain't balled out all on a nigga in a while. She was brought out of her thoughts by the cashier saying, "Will this be all, ma'am?" She nodded yes and watched as Darryl pulled out at least five to six bands from one pocket. All that was running through her mind was "cha-ching." At that moment it was like Darryl read her mind.

"I know what you thinking but fallback, ma. It ain't tricking if you got it." He smiled as he helped her carry her bags out the store as they headed out to do more destruction.

Not only were the guys buying Taz and Veronica everything they wanted, they were also buying themselves a lot of stuff, too; from Gucci shoes to Hudson, Balmain jeans, hats and everything in between. Rain, who was Veronica's sponsor in the mall, even purchased a $6,000 watch from one of the top jewelry stores in the mall. Veronica was impressed. This was her first time ever being treated like this. Her kids' father, Dre, definitely never did anything this nice for her. The best he could do was buy her some Church's chicken and that was every now and then. And Veronica was thinking how she liked hanging with Taz and how cool she was. She was impressed by the company Taz attracted.

After hitting a few more stores, Darryl pulled Taz aside and said, "Damn ma, you just set me back a couple grand."

"What did you expect?" Taz replied. "You could tell when you first laid eyes on me I was going to run your check up." They both started laughing.

Darryl said, "Yeah, I could tell. I really don't want you to have to pay for anything this entire trip. I want you to be my baby for the entire weekend."

Taz replied, "You need to be specific in what you're asking for because I don't play games and something tells me that you definitely want me to give you a little more than my time. So stop playing games and say what you got to say."

"Damn baby girl," Darryl said, "pump your brakes. I'm sure you can see I'm not pressed for a woman. I just think you're really cool and being that I live in New York and you live in Georgia, I want to spend as much time as possible with you while we are here."

"So you came all the way to Houston to get booed up?" Taz asked.

Darryl laughed. "No baby, I'ma let you do you and I'ma do me. But since I'm feeling you I just wanted to let you know up front that you don't have to pay for anything all weekend. Is that too much to ask Ms. Tashawn?" Taz smiled at him and winked and they continued to shop throughout the Galleria Mall.

* * * * * * * * *

Meanwhile, on the other side of the mall Lola was doing her thing solo. She had taken Taz's advice and decided to keep her bad attitude to herself. She went into a few stores and did a little damage. She wasn't about to risk her baller seeing her in the mall walking with some other dude looking like some low budget groupie. She was already in the doghouse for popping up in Houston knowing this was the wifey's weekend. At first, Lola was comfortable with her position. But as she became more attached to him she got tired of being the sidepiece to one of the top retired NBA players. Even though he was married he paid to play and was very generous and nice to Lola when she would act right. Lola was not about to lose this guy.

After long conversations about his current relationship Lola discovered not only was his wife lazy, but she was a coldhearted bitch who was responsible for causing her husband's retirement. From what Lola knew the wifey suspected her husband of cheating and one day decided to play detective. While lying in backseat of his SUV one Sunday afternoon, she plotted to hop out at his final destination which she thought would be some bitch's house. While he was on his cell phone getting directions, she couldn't hold it in any longer and when he ended the conversation with, "I love you too, baby. See you soon," the wifey—who was not small herself at 5'9" and 160 pounds—jumped up from behind the backseat, screaming and swinging. Caught off guard with one hand on the steering wheel and the other on his cell phone, the now retired NBA player lost control of the vehicle and crashed, hitting a car with a family of four. Everyone was killed which included two adults and two small children. After two months in a temporary coma and multiple surgeries he was told he would never play again due to his leg and back injuries as well as his constant migraines and seizures.

When the story hit the airwaves America felt sorry for him because his wife made up a story about him blacking out while driving. After he was out of the hospital he revealed to her who she "thought" was his secret lover. She was actually his long lost sister that had located him on Facebook. He had been separated from her since the age of 12. However, if the media had ever found out that the cause of their family's death was a case of stupidity and domestic disputes, his legacy and his career would have been ruined. To this day he felt nothing but anger towards his wife who always threw in his face that she was not the one who killed a family of four, he was. He knew if he ever divorced her, the truth would come out. And even though he was not at fault he would definitely be the one to take the fall. While feeling sorry for him, Lola had done the ultimate no-no. She had fallen hard for this guy.

* * * * * * * * * *

Veronica, who at this point of her trip was already missing her two daughters, held a brief conversation with the guy she was walking with through the mall. She noticed he would constantly look over his shoulder and kept his fitted hat low over his eyes. Even though this guy, who called himself Rain, was completely different from Dre, she had to admit his thug appeal was sexy; and if she wasn't so wrapped up in Dre's bullshit she would have loved to let him Rain all over her. Rain stood 6'2" and was darker than dark. He slightly favored the model, Tyson Beckford, was a little more on the muscular side. The way he sported his Chicago Bulls fitted over his waves made him look as if though he was hiding his eyes which were already covered with D&G shades. He had on an all-white Polo V-neck sweater with red trimming and at least enough ice to give Gucci Mane a run for his money. He knew how to wear his Polo plaid shorts, not sagging too much but not too preppy. He was wearing his all-white number 13 Jordan's that added that flavor which said "trapper of the year."

"So Veronica, tell ya boy what the ATL feeling like right now. I ain't been in a few months." Rain stepped in closer as they walked through the mall, trying to wrap his arm around Veronica's waist.

"Uh unh, boo. This ain't even that type of party. You a little too comfortable. She politely removed his arm from around her waist and said, "And the ATL is still hot and poppin' and waiting for me to come back to attend to my kids and H-U-S-B-A-N-D," she said, dragging out the last word, lifting her wedding ring finger that had a fake wedding ring on it that she used as roach spray against bug-a-boos.

Rain stopped in the middle of the mall and started laughing out loud. "Ha-ha! You serious, girl that ain't no wedding ring. That ain't even an engagement ring. You silly-ass bitches really be trying to run game." He was bent over, laughing his ass off.

Veronica stood frozen with her hand on her hip not believing her ears. "I know you ain't fixed your raggedy-ass mouth to call me no bitch cause nigga I'll let this whole can of mace rain on your ass." Veronica held up her miniature keychain size can of mace that was in a pink princess cut diamond leather case. But for some reason when Rain called her a bitch it made her pussy wet. His thug appeal was just so appealing.

"Look baby girl, you with Rain and this is how I roll. I don't care who you with, married to or fucking on the side. I'm just trying to show you a good time. But don't get it fucked up. You keep up that lil jazzy preacher's wife shit and I'm out." Rain walked off and left Veronica standing in the middle of the mall.

Veronica bit her tongue and thought, "Fuck it. Shit I came to Houston to get away from bullshit and drama and now this lil conceited-ass nigga got a bitch ready to fly back to her boring-ass baby-daddy. But fuck it, I'm going to enjoy my time and his pockets." Veronica started walking fast as she sped up to catch him. "Rain, Rain you right, I'm tripping, boo. You running the show."

Rain smiled like he had just checkmated her in chess. "Yeah, you can Twitter Rihanna and tell her to loan you her umbrella cause it's about to Rain," he told her as they walked into the Footlocker. What neither of them knew was that this weekend was going to be the craziest weekend of both their lives.

CHAPTER 21

"Yes, another Georgia Peach, please?" Taz asked the waitress. She was on her third round of drinks. Veronica just looked at her and laughed. They were at the Cheesecake Factory inside the Galleria Mall and about to eat before they headed back to their hotel rooms. Darryl and Rain had shown them some real hospitality at the mall and wanted to feed the young ladies before they departed ways.

"Yo', what's up with shawty who was in the back seat? She think she too good to spend a nigga money or something?" asked Sosa. He was the one in the passenger seat of the Bentley. He had anticipated spending a few dollars on Lola but to his surprise she was nowhere to be found when it was time to shop.

"She's going through a little something right now," Taz said. "Don't worry; she'll give you some time before the weekend is over."

"Before the weekend is over? She must be here with her dude or something?" Sosa replied.

"No, no not at all," Veronica said as she sipped on her Apple Martini.

At that moment, Taz's cell phone rang. It's Lola. "Hello," Taz said.

"Hi Taz, where are you guys?" asked Lola.

"We're at the Cheesecake Factory, sitting all the way in the back. Meet us here."

The phone in Darryl's pocket rang and the ringtone interrupted the casual conversation at the table. "Excuse me for a minute, ladies," Darryl said and stood up to take his call. "I'll be a second or two. Order another round of drinks until I return."

As Darryl walked away from the table Taz eyed him with suspicion, thinking to herself, "Uh uh, niggas are all the same."

What none of them knew was that the Bryson Tiller R&B ringtone was a throw-off. The call was actually one of his loyal customers that he had been supplying work to for quite some time. As he strolled out the restaurant, he noticed the sun was blazing and reminded himself he needed to get the Bentley buffed and waxed one more time today before the fun jumped off. "Talk to me." This was his signature greeting he always use when answering the phone. The caller on the other end was glad to reach his connect.

"Mane, I'm happy I caught yo' ass, dawg. Mane, before y'all get to stunting too hard this week the streets still gotta eat. So I'ma need a quick nine-piece nugget to fill up my appetite."

The dude on the other end was named Yung, one of Darryl's lil niggas he had raised in the hood many years ago and kept out of trouble. "Don't trip lil nigga. I'ma have my folks go to McDonald's and pick that order up for you. But do me a favor, instead of giving them the money, I need you to drop it off downtown for me at a special location. Grab a pen and paper so I can tell you whose name to leave it in." Darryl was about to get his stunt on big time and if this worked out, he was about to add another shawty to his team. "I'm about to text you the name now." After hanging up his phone he texted Yung and also texted his folks and told them his youngin was starving and wanted a nine-piece nugget from McDonald's. He told them he was paying for it which really meant that Darryl was fronting him the package on consignment. That way once his folks dropped it off they didn't expect any money. Life for Darryl wasn't always this good.

* * * * * * * * *

"Pass the ball, nigga. I'm wide open!" yelled Darryl Washington to his best friend Rico who became irritated.

"Fuck this nigga. He the star of the team," Rico whispered to himself. "He already got a scholarship. I got to do me or I'ma be stuck in the hood for life. Look at all these college scouts." So Rico drove the ball up court, pulled up and drained a long range three-pointer which brought his team within one point with only 30 seconds left on the clock.

"Time Out!" the other high school coach yelled as his team rallied around him. However, on the other end of the court shit was crazy.

"Fuck nigga, you trying to steal my shine. Nigga you see the scouts out there; they came to see me D. Dub, Big D, not you. Nigga, you acting like you Jordan when you really just a Scottie Pippen." Darryl shoved his finger in Rico's chest as he spoke angrily.

"Guys, guys calm down. He's right Rico, pass the ball. The game is on the line. That last shot you took was risky and this is the championship game. All of you are seniors and if you lose this, there will be no next year," Coach Ramsey said, looking Rico Taylor in the eyes. Rico was a good kid, just troubled. He thought that since his father was a high school legend he was supposed to fill his shoes. Truth was —he couldn't. The coach had raised his father and felt sorry for his kid after he died and gave Rico the last spot on the team. But he damn sure was not about to let Rico fuck up Darryl Washington's scholarship to big name schools like Duke, Baylor, Georgetown, Michigan State and Indiana University. Coach Ramsey knew true talent and Darryl Washington was the next big thing. Maybe not Jordan, but he was definitely a Magic Johnson.

"You hear that, nigga? Pass me the ball. I got us here; me not you. So do your job and when I get in the NBA I might get you a ball boy job or something."

Before Rico could counterattack the buzzer sounded, alerting both teams that the one minute timeout was over. Rico had made his mind up. He was thinking, "If I get the ball, I'm gone shoot it. My life is already fucked up and I ain't about to let this nigga think he the reason I went anywhere."

As the other team inbounded the ball time started ticking almost as if in slow motion. The point guard of the team held on to the ball knowing that with a one-point lead all they had to do was run the time down and force a foul. But Rico wanted to be a star. As the point guard drove to the basket he slipped and lost the ball. There was 20 seconds left and both Darryl and Rico saw the loose ball and run for it. With 18 seconds left, Rico had full control of the ball until he's stripped by none other than Darryl Washington, his own teammate. The clock is at 16 seconds and Rico runs down the court and sets up position underneath the goal, wide open! Now with 12 seconds left, Darryl looks to the bench and the coach gives him two thumbs down which meant "shove it down their throats."

"D.Dub, pass the rock. I'm wide open bruh!" Rico yelled.

All of the offensive players were triple-teaming the star and the state's best shooter, Darryl Washington. With 7 seconds to go, Darryl dribbles to his left, shake's two defenders then crosses over to the right. It's down to 4 seconds and he pushes the ball through the free throw line, and with 2 seconds left he lifts up into the air and at the final 1 second he dunks the ball with both hands, scores and the game is over! The gym erupts and all the high school kids and his teammates surround Darryl like he's some sort of God

The local news reporters are in absolute awe as they continued to replay the phenomenal game-winning dunk. After being worshipped like the Messiah he took a minute to breathe and answer the news anchors' questions.

"So Darryl, what's for you now?" the smiling Korean lady asked, standing next to the sweaty star.

"The sky's the limit! Hey mom! Hey grandma! Wow!" After his brief interview he made his way to the locker room to celebrate with the team. When he walked into the musty locker room the coach held the State Championship trophy in his hand and looked up.

"Boy, get yo' ass over here and touch this. Damn boy, I ain't never seen no one as good as you!"

Rico was still upset that he didn't get the last shot so he decided to sit by his locker. After hearing the coach's last remark he lost it. He opened his locker and pulled out his Wilson gym bag. He reached into it slowly and pulled out a chrome nine millimeter gun. He walked up to the crowd of players who were still caught up in the moment. When the coach looked up he was too late. *"Nooo…!"*

Rico shot the coach twice, hitting him in the leg and upper chest area. He aimed recklessly, trying to shoot one person, his biggest shot of the day, Darryl Washington. In the midst of trying to shoot Darryl, Rico shot, injured and killed three more players. While trying to get out of the crowded and panicked locker room Darryl was trapped by the body of his fallen coach.

"Nigga, all you had to do was pass the ball." Rico said in a calm voice. *"I was wide open. We could have both went to the top. Nigga, your family ain't poor like mines. Your momma ain't cracked out like mines. Your daddy didn't have AIDS. Nigga you always been about one person —* YOU!"

Darryl couldn't believe his ears. Rico really hated him. *"You gone kill me cause I want to win, because my parents are blessed, or because you hate me, Rico? Which one?"* You could hear sirens outside the school's gymnasium and the screech of police cars. This was like a dream with their coach's bloody body at his feet and other dead or injured bodies littered the locker room floor.

Darryl wondered if he was just asleep and having a nightmare. But this was no nightmare because both he and Rico were crying.

"Naw, I ain't gone kill you," Rico replied as he aimed at Darryl's left knee and squeezed the trigger. Darryl screamed at the impact of the bullet and grabbed at his knee. Rico quickly shot him in his right leg and Darryl screamed again, slumping to the ground. Then Rico pointed the gun to his head.

"I loved you like a brother. I would never kill you but you gone remember this until the day you die." Then Rico pulled the trigger and blew his brains out all over the locker room floor.

Rico was right. Darryl has never forgotten that night. He made a quick recovery in time for his first year at Duke, but he vowed to never, ever play basketball again in his life; never again.

* * * * * * * * *

A few minutes after her call to Taz, Lola arrived at the table. She was carrying about five shopping bags. Rain walked in too and bursts out singing, *"Where in the world is Carmen San Diego?"* The entire table starts laughing hysterically and Lola, who tried not to laugh, couldn't help but join in as well. The girls finished up their drinks and dinner and told the guys goodbye. Darryl came back to tell everyone goodbye as well because he had to leave and pick someone up from the airport. Sosa and Rain didn't go with him because they had more shopping to do and were enjoying their small talk with Lola and Veronica.

Later as the girls walked to the truck they were wasted. They were laughing, slurring words, stumbling and talking loud as hell. Taz and Veronica had so many bags they could barely carry them all. Lola was surprised as hell once she saw them with so many bags.

"Damn, did Darryl and Rain buy all of that?" Lola asked.

"Yep, every last piece of it," replied Veronica.

When the girls got to the hotel they all agreed they were tired and needed a nap. So Veronica went to her room and Taz and Lola went to the suite. Once there Lola was very anxious to find an outlet and charge up her phone. It had gone dead at the mall and she hoped to God she hadn't missed Michael's phone call. She pulled out her charger and plugged her phone up in her room, turned it on and stared at the screen, desperately hoping that she would see the indicator that she had a text or voicemail message. However, nothing was there. She sighed and started unpacking her bag in preparation for her nap.

"Why the long face?" Taz asked as she comes out of the bathroom into Lola's room. "Let me guess, he hasn't called or texted you, huh?" Lola just lay there with a blank look of disgust on her face. "The chances of him contacting you are slim to none, Lola. You already said you had no business being down here because he is with his wife. He didn't get you a room or a rental car and he is not answering your calls or texts. That means he's not worried about your wellbeing and could care less what you are doing or even if you're okay. His focus is on his family right now. I know it's easier said than done, but you are going to have to let him go for the weekend if you want to enjoy yourself."

In her room, Veronica rushed out of the shower to try and answer the phone. As she dried off her hands she looked at the phone screen and saw she'd missed seven calls from Dre. She rolled her eyes and decided to call him back. She's wondering if maybe it's not him calling. Maybe it's the girls calling, wanting to talk to me.

Oh well, Veronica soon found out it wasn't her girls because Dre answered. "Why in the fuck you ain't been answering this muthafucking phone?" snaps Dre.

"Umm hello, excuse me," Veronica replied.

"You heard what the hell I asked. I been calling you for thirty minutes and I want to know why I couldn't get in contact with you," yelled Dre.

"Damn Dre, I been in the shower. I didn't hear the phone ringing until I just got out. Stop calling and trying to check on me, okay? Where are Sariyah and McKenzie?" Veronica snapped back.

"I shouldn't let your unfit ass talk to them. You think you so fucking slick. My big homie hit me and told me he saw you in the Cheesecake Factory in Houston, Texas with a group of hoes. He said its All-Star weekend out there. So you a groupie now? You leave your fucking kids on me all weekend to go run behind NBA players?" Dre complained.

"Dre, first of all, those are not just my fucking kids. They belong to you, too, nigga. Secondly, yes, you're correct. I am in Houston and I was at the Cheesecake Factory, but I swear to God I did not know it was NBA All-Star weekend until I got here," said Veronica.

"Shut the hell up lying with yo' lying ass. You told me you were going to a class for that raggedy-ass daycare you trying to open. But your trick-ass all the way in Houston, running behind niggas. I outta tell your daughters how full of shit you are, but I'm going to handle you myself when you get back," he threatened.

Veronica just looked at the phone and said, "Goodbye Dre. I need to get off the phone. I have so much tricking to do that your time on this phone call has expired. Grow up, and I will come directly over to pick up our daughters when I make it back to Atlanta." Then she hung up on Dre and started rolling a much needed blunt.

Downstairs, Taz made her way to the front desk. She had received a call from customer service saying she had a package at the front desk waiting for her. She was very confused because no one knew where she was staying except her friends back home in Atlanta, and she knew none of them had been generous enough to surprise her with something. So as she walked to the front desk she was nervous. "Hi, I'm Tashawn Vasquez in Room 2518. I was told there was a package for me," Taz said in a puzzled voice. The front desk clerk handed Taz a large manila envelope taped and secured very tightly. There was a note on the envelope which read, "Do not open until you get to your room." At this point Taz's heart was about to fall out of her chest. She was scared.

* * * * * * * * *

Toney looked at Taz like she was a piece of steak meat with his glassy, cracked-out pupils. "Girl, come over here and give daddy some sugar." Taz looked at him weirdly and said, "You ain't my daddy. My daddy in heaven and he know God and he gone come and get me one day and he gone let me fly to heaven…"

"Bitch! I didn't ask you about your punk-ass daddy did I? I'm your new daddy, okay? Now come on over here and give me a kiss."

Taz started to cry. She wondered why her mom hadn't come into the room and checked on her. And what was that funky smell in the air?" But as she walked over and kissed Toney on the cheek, Thelma walked in. "What the fuck?" she said.

Toney, caught off guard tried to explain. "Naw baby, it ain't what it look like."

Thelma put her hands on her hips and said, "Nigga, I know what it looks like. It looks like that fast-ass hussie trying to steal my man. Toney go in there and fix the pipe. I cracked it." Toney hurried up and rushed out the room. He was so caught up he had forgotten all about the dope. Thelma threw her nappy hair back and looked at Taz like Medusa. "Listen you little fast-ass heifer. That's my man, okay? Let's get that straight. I don't want your ass near him."

Taz was confused. "But mommy he told me to."

Thelma reared her hand back and slapped the shit out of Taz and then began to choke her as she shouted, "Bitch that's my man!" When she let go she looked at Taz's little body as it heaved up and down as she cried. "And clean up this room before I really give your ass something to cry about." As Thelma walked out the room she stopped as if in thought and came back into the room. Taz thought her mommy was about to apologize, hug her and wipe away her tears. Instead, Thelma whispered, "Oh yeah, and the next time I catch you all in my man's face, I'ma kill you." Thelma slammed the door on her way out and went to her room where she gave Toney head while he gave the glass dick some head. "I'm sorry about that crazy-ass child. She lonely and jealous." Soon Thelma was lost in dreamland.

Taz cried and cried. "Daddy, when you gone come and get me? You 'pose to let me fly to heaven with you like grandma said." Taz's daddy had been a young boss who once had Hollywood Courts projects sewed up. He gave his daughter everything a ghetto child could ever want. When he got shot on her third birthday at The Varsity—a fast-food hot dog spot in Atlanta—Taz's life was changed from better to worse.

CHAPTER 22

While sitting at the bar in the lobby of the Hotel Derek, Veronica was sipping on a sex-on-the-beach followed by a shot of Patrón as she contemplated which one of her new outfits she would put on tonight. She had this badass BCBG dress that she knew would be a showstopper. This dress was smoking. It was a crocodile-print, black and white body dress that showed off every one of Veronica's curves. It stopped at mid-thigh and showed lots of cleavage. She was sure to look fierce and turn lots of heads if she decided to wear this dress. Paired with the Christian Louboutin red bottom heels Rain had bought her she was confident that her first night in Houston would definitely be one to remember.

As she ordered another sex-on the-beach she noticed a handsome young man walk into the bar by himself. He was a cutie and definitely Veronica's type. He was about 6'3" with very dark chocolate skin, nice pearly white teeth and a mouth full of icy white diamonds. Veronica was instantly turned on. She was thinking that this dude was fine and guessed he was from Texas with that icy white grill. She knew she needed to get this guy's attention. But instead of walking over to him, she decided to do something a little bossier. Veronica asked the waitress that had just tended to him a shot of Patrón, a shot of Hennessey and a Corona with lime from her.

When the waitress brought the drinks to the gentleman's table, he told her, "No little mama, this is all wrong. I didn't order any drinks."

"I know you didn't," the waitress replied. "These drinks are courtesy of the pretty black girl sitting at the bar. She wasn't sure what you liked to drink so she decided to send you a little bit of everything. Should I send the drinks back?"

"Absolutely not!" responded the young man. "If a woman that pretty can buy me a drink then the least I can do is drink it."

The waitress smiled and continued to set the drinks up on his table and when she finished she headed back over to Veronica. Veronica wasn't sure what she'd just done because she had never been that bold. But she damn sure could get used to it. She felt like a "real boss bitch." She definitely liked Houston already.

After sipping on each of the drinks Veronica had sent over, Slim got up and walked over to the bar to join her. "I've never mixed white and brown liquor nor do I drink Corona. But a woman as fine as you sent them so I had to drink all three," Slim said as he took the seat next to Veronica. "What's your name, beautiful? I'm Slim, Texas Slim to be exact."

Veronica looked him up and down and replied, "I'm Veronica and trust me, the pleasure's all mine."

"I can tell by that sexy, southern accent you definitely not from Texas. Where you from baby girl?" asked Slim.

Veronica blushed. "I'm from Atlanta, Slim. Maybe you can show me around Houston if you're not too busy."

"I'll drink to that, Choco. I can already tell I'd like to do much more than show you round."

"Choco? What the hell does Choco mean? Is that some type of Texas slang?" asked Veronica.

"No, baby girl. Choco is short for chocolate and from now on that's what I'm calling you. I sure hope you can get used to it."

As Slim eyeballed his new catch he remembered he had to hit his brother and his crew off with a few more pounds of purp. His lil brother's click were up and coming hustlers but they were sloppy. They boasted, bragged, flossed and put their business in the streets too much. It was hard to show niggas who never had anything how to get something. Plus, Slim's lil brother was what you would call an ex-goon. He used to rob niggas for jewelry, weight, whips, rims and whatever, you name it. But after a short prison stint Slim decided to bring lil bruh on. He excused himself for a moment and walked a short distance away from Veronica as he dialed his lil bruh's number. He heard his baby bruh's voice after the second ring.

"Bruh, bruh what's up on your end?"

Slim laughed. His lil brother had swag potential. "It's all to the G.; just enjoying my life with a new trophy. But what's up with you? Did your plane land safely? Nigga, you know its terrorists everywhere. And since they killed Bin-Bin and been wiping down shit over there its trippin'." Slim kept looking at Veronica while she finished her drink. She looked over at him and he gave her the "one minute signal" with is finger to let her know he was wrapping up his call.

"Nawl, we good. Me and Drill copped a rental and we on our way to a hotel right now to check-in. After we get situated I'ma buzz you back and talk numbers."

Slim ended the call and walked back to the bar and slid into his seat beside Veronica. "Now, where were we?"

* * * * * * * * *

"You lil funky bitch! You with me now, you hear? My rule is easy: do what I say, whatever I say you do and don't speak unless spoken to. These

is Big Mama's rules. You the foster bastard child and I'm the muthafucka paying bills and taking care of you, you little fucker. You got that?" Big Mama—whose real name was Sue—popped Veronica in the back of the head after giving her the same speech she had heard over and over again.

"Why you so mean? I don't ever be mean to you. I just want my dad…"

On the last word Big Mama punched her in the mouth with a closed fist. "Bitch, you getting sassy with me?"

Veronica started crying and shaking her head, no, as she tried to wipe away the blood from the small cut her teeth made inside her mouth from the punch. Big Mama stood at 6'2" and weighed a hefty 350 pounds. She was too fat for regular clothing so she wore a muumuu that looked like a big-ass sheet with flowers on it. "I'll tell you what, I'ma give you something to put in ya mouth since you can't keep the muthafucka closed. Bring yo' ass here." Veronica knew what time it was as she walked slowly toward the couch. Big Mama sat down and gave her a bowl of dog food. She watched the child eat the dog food and felt powerful. Then she forced the child to perform oral sex acts on her. After she was satisfied, she slapped Veronica hard across the face and said, "Now go to bed, bitch."

This behavior is common in America's foster homes: child abuse, rape, sexual molestation, mistreatment, etc.

CHAPTER 23

B ack in the room, Lola was on the internet trying her best to find out where Michael was going to have his "Welcome to Houston" All-Star weekend party. She was one hundred percent sure this party was going to take place because for the past two years she had been the piece on his arm at this event while he and his wife had been on rocky terms. This was not a public invite event. This event always included the NBA's elite and those prominent in the NBA. So now, after an unsuccessful search, she knew she was going to have to pull some strings to find out the location of this private affair. One thing Lola knew and that was that ballers hung out with ballers. She knew that to find out the whereabouts of this event, she was going to have to spark up an old flame.

And while on the elevator to the 25th floor, it stops at floor 17 and Veronica walks into the elevator. She was clearly drunk and looked puzzled when she saw Taz already on the elevator. "Where are you sneaking in from?" Veronica asked her in a slightly slurred voice.

"No, the question is where are you sneaking in from? You're staying on the 22nd floor so why the hell are you getting on at the 17th floor?" Taz asked. But without waiting on an answer she said, "But any who girl, I'm about to shit in my pants. I get a call from the front desk saying I have a package waiting on me but no one knows I'm staying here. Girl, I'm scared shitless."

"Hmmm, that's very weird," Veronica replied leaning against the wall of the elevator to stay upright. "Well, I'm headed to your room to get some toothpaste. Lola gave me the okay to come get some of hers, so I guess we will see what's in this mystery package when we get to the room."

When the girls walked into the living room of the suite they noticed Lola hurriedly hung up the phone. "Damn, did we interrupt your phone conversation?" asked Taz as she and Veronica plop down onto the couch.

"Don't let me worry you," Lola replied. "Let's talk about what's in that envelope," she laughed, pointing at it lying on Taz's lap.

But Taz decided to open the envelope alone in case there was something in it she didn't want the girls to see. So she got up and took it with her into the bathroom. Once she locked the door she took several deep breaths and decided to go ahead and open it. She unraveled all the tape and finally got the flap of the envelope open. As she was about to peek inside, she was interrupted by loud banging on the bathroom door.

"Police bitch! Open up!" yelled Lola and Veronica as they burst out laughing.

"Damn bitches, stop playing. I was just about to look in it until you guys scared the shit out of me. My heart is about to jump out of my damn chest."

"Okay, okay bitch, but hurry up. We're anxious as hell, too, ya know." The girls walked back into the living room of the suite, giggling and laughing to wait patiently on the couch.

A few moments later Taz came out of the bathroom with the biggest grin on her face. "Damn, what was in the package? What the hell are you smiling for?" demanded Lola.

"All I want to know is which one of you bitches told Darryl what hotel I was staying in?" Taz asked with a smile.

"Oh yeah, um, that would be me," Veronica replied quietly. "When we were in the Gucci store, I was on Google, looking and searching for the number to the hotel. He was right there so he must have been peeping over my shoulder. Is that who the package is from?"

"Girl, hell yes!" Taz responded.

"Well, what the hell is in it?" snapped Lola.

"Girl, nothing. It's just a little something to let me know I was on his mind," Taz said.

"Look sweetie, I know you don't know us but you can play them type of games with someone else. You just meet this nigga and he's obviously a boss of some sort. There're only two things that could be in that package: number 1, money or number 2, drugs. And if I'm going to be staying in this suite with you, I damn sure hope that you would have enough respect to let me know what's in the room where I'm laying my head," Lola said, acting like she was a boss.

Taz walked across the room and put her envelope into the hotel safe. Then she aggressively walked over to Lola and said, nastily, "Look bitch, let's get a couple of things straight. I don't owe you an explanation about shit! This is my room bought with my money so even if I had 10 bricks in this muthafucka, it wouldn't be a damn thing you could do or say about it. That package said "Tashawn" muthafucking "Vasquez" on the front of it. It don't say "Lola" nowhere on the muthafucka. So stay in your lane and let me handle my shit. You don't have to stay here. Bitch, if you don't feel comfortable you're more than welcome to leave. There's the front door bitch, bye!"

Lola's face had turned a fire-engine red. She jumped up and started snatching up some of her belongings in the living room.

But she just had to snap back. "Bitch, who the fuck you talking to? I done spared your ass a couple of times with that smart-ass, slick-ass mouth of yours. Don't think cause you let me stay in this raggedy-ass muthafucking hotel room that a bitch owe you something. I'm a made bitch, been a made bitch. You just a bitch down here trying to get drafted. Bitch, I been drafted and I come off the bench frequently. Step ya game up and sex ya frame up and then step to a bad bitch like me with that reckless-ass bullshit that comes out your mouth!"

Then Lola stomped into the bedroom and stuffed everything into her piece of luggage. As Taz struggled to recover and get a few words in, Lola was out the door with all her belongings, headed toward the elevator. Taz had finally met her match.

* * * * * * * * *

Lola looked at the chalkboard but kept turning her head to look at the clock on the blue and yellow wall of her 7th grade classroom. At twelve years old, Lola still had the body and size of a seven-year old girl. Her fingers were always red from first, biting off the nails, and then the skin around them. She did this whenever a certain date popped up on the calendar. Today was visiting day at Grady hospital. This was where her mother, Sara, had been held the past couple of years, going through extensive psychiatric evaluations for paranoia and schizophrenia in conjunction with a list of other mental illnesses she was diagnosed with after the death of Lola's father, Lonis. The doctors privately believed Sara's mind just "cracked" after witnessing the brutality of her husband's death. But in reality, Sara's mind "cracked" from her treatments at the mental hospital she was transferred from.

Sara's mother and father had taken Lola in after her father's side of the family disowned her. They packed up and moved to Atlanta after receiving hundreds of death threats. The burning cross in her Grandpa John's yard was the final straw. After relocating to Lithonia—a suburb of

Atlanta—Lola thought things would be better, which they were just not all the time.

"Agggghh!!…Agggghh!! Daddy no! Please don't shoot my daddy no more, please! Agggghh!!…help my daddy…mommy, help daddy….Agggghh! Agggghh! Agggghh!" Lola shook uncontrollably in her sleep. She was drenched in sweat and her own urine.

After hearing her scream, her Grandpa John ran into her room with his rifle. "Baby, Lo-Lo, honey sugar, snap out of it. Papa's here, okay? See, I got my gun. Ain't nobody gonna hurt you no more."

This was the fifth night Lola had awakened like this. The only thing that calmed her down was papa and his rifle. Her Grandpa John stood a mere 5'11" with a beer belly that could have fit Santa Claus. He kept his hair razor-shaved with a nicely trimmed goatee. He had zero tolerance for any bullshit but he was loving and caring with his Lo-Lo.

Lola always asked him, "Papa, are you gonna teach me how to shoot your gun so I can get the bad guys?"

Papa would laugh and say, "Yes baby, I'm gonna teach you how to get 'em. Let's get you cleaned up and then you can go back to sleep. I'm here now."

After the sound of the class bell, Lola walked out of the class and outside her Jr. high school and opened the door of her grandpa's Cadillac. "Hey pudding pie how was class today?" he always asked.

"Boring, but I learned something new," Lola always replied.

"Well baby, you know today we got to see your mother like always. If you don't want to go you don't have to. It's your choice. You're old enough to make your own decisions."

And Lola always replied, "Yes, I'll go." What bothered her was every time she visited the gray-haired woman they said was her mother it was like her mom was a zombie. "Mommy, it's me, Lola."

But her mom just stared and said, "I love Lonis. Why would anyone hurt my baby?"

Although Lola really didn't want to go see her mother, she knew it made her grandpa happy, especially after losing his wife and her grandmother two years prior. After Lola saw how losing her father affected her mother, she vowed to never make friends or have a serious lover. She knew if it was possible for a father to have his own son brutally murdered then the niggas and bitches in the streets would definitely have no mercy on her.

* * * * * * * * *

Taz and Veronica agreed to meet in the lobby at 11:45 to hit the streets that night. Slim had called Veronica and wanted her to meet him at an exclusive NBA party which would be held downtown at the Four Seasons Hotel in Houston. Veronica couldn't help feeling bad for Lola and was desperately trying to contact her. She could see why both women were upset but first and foremost she wanted to make sure Lola was okay.

"Fuck that bitch. She's a grown-ass woman. Ain't nobody 'bout to kiss her ass," snapped Taz as they walked to the truck. Taz was looking as fly as a supermodel. She had on a tight, knee-length orange, cream and gold satin Versace dress that showed each and every one of Taz's assets. She was wearing it with a pair of Giuseppe Zanotti heels. She was dressed to kill. She had paired the outfit with a nice gold Versace clutch and fire-red lips which tied her hair color into the dress. After Veronica had told Taz that it was an exclusive NBA event she knew she had to step her game up for the night. She looked fierce. She didn't want to wear anything too short and sleazy and look like a groupie. There would be player's wives there and she wanted to look just as classy as any of them. While Taz wasn't going to the event looking for a baller, she damn sure wasn't opposed to them looking for her.

Veronica had the good girl look about her for the night. She kept it simple with a nice mid-thigh, black cocktail dress paired with a pair of gold Gucci heels and matching clutch. She had on just a tad bit of makeup with nude color lips to tie the outfit together. Veronica was digging Slim so she decided to downplay her look. She didn't want any other guy looking at her tonight; she had her eye on Slim.

As the girls rode through the city of Houston, listening to Philthy Phil's new mix-tape and talking, all Taz could think about was the package Darryl left for her at the front desk. She wasn't quite sure how to feel about it. While it was very generous, and she had no thoughts of giving it back, she couldn't figure out if it was just Darryl trying to stunt, or if he had some ulterior motive. One thing Taz did learn about Veronica from the entire package ordeal was that she respected people's privacy. Once Veronica saw that Taz wasn't interested in sharing the contents of the package, she'd backed away and didn't question her about it again. Taz really respected that. But that bitch, Lola, she figured was a nosy, jealous bitch that she was definitely going to have to watch in the event she ever came back. *"I fuck with gorillas, I fuck with gorillas…"* the song blasted out of the speakers. That's exactly how Taz felt at the moment.

When the ladies pulled up in front of the hotel, they could definitely see this was the party to be at. In the valet and regular parking lots there was nothing but Bentleys, Range Rovers, Ferrari's, Escalades, Rolls Royce Wraiths and any other high-end car that was in style pulling in, trying to park. The girls got out of the truck and walked toward the lobby of the hotel to wait for Slim. This was an invite-only party and apparently Slim had some pull because you had to either be staying at the hotel or be on the guest list to get into the party. Veronica and Taz walked over to the hostess at the lobby door and Veronica politely said, "Hi, we're on the list —Veronica Paris and Tashawn Vasquez." The hostess scrolled to page three of the guest list on her iPad and sure enough they were on the list. She unhooked the red velvet rope, which had the entrance to the lobby blocked off, from the stanchion and let the ladies through.

"Girl, was that Mary J. Blige we just walked past?" Veronica asked Taz.

"Yes girl it was. Don't she look good?" Taz replied.

The girls made their way over to the bar and luckily found two seats. "I sure wish I had something to puff on right about now," laughed Veronica.

"Oh, what? You nervous about meeting your boo? Don't be scurred, girl," Taz joked. "By the way, tell me again where you met this dude? I damn near been with you the entire time since you got to Houston and I ain't heard you mention nothing 'bout no nigga named Slim."

Veronica blushed and said, "Girl, I met him in the hotel when I went downstairs to get a drink after we came back from the mall, and he was there. I don't know what your type is but this brother is fine. I definitely hope he has the personality to match."

Taz smiled at Veronica. "Girl, you know that's why I like you. You just go with the flow and don't walk around with your nose all stuck in the air like you shit. I'm sure that you could if you wanted to. You're a beautiful girl, nice body and obviously have some cash flow to blow cause you're here in Houston; but you act like a cool, down to earth chick. It's nice to finally meet someone with some substance. NO HOMO so let me throw that disclaimer out there, but you're cool. I'm glad we met at the airport, girl. We are about to have some fun this weekend," Taz said excitedly.

CHAPTER 24

Lola had found her credit card while the girls were shopping at the Galleria and had no intentions of staying in Taz's room the entire weekend anyway. Her plans were to wake up the next morning and march right back down to the front desk and get her own room. So after she stormed out of Taz's room she went downstairs to the front desk and managed to get a room that someone cancelled at the last minute. Lola had never been the type to get along with too many females, especially ones that she didn't know. The moment Taz had made her proposal she already knew that the arrangement of them staying together wasn't going to last long. She still wondered why that bitch was acting so secretive about that package. For all she knew, the bitch could be moving weight right under her nose. She wasn't about to lay her head in a room where a bitch was getting mysterious packages from a nigga she just met. What part of the game is that?

Lola had found out from one of her dudes named Smoke where Michael was having his "Welcome to Houston" party. She'd hated to call Smoke and ask him for anything because Smoke was the type to always want something in return. However, she was desperate and knew in order to find out the address she had to suck up her pride. So Lola had gotten to the hotel extremely early. She knew she couldn't arrive late because it was an invitation-only party. If she waited too late she would be among hundreds of others trying to talk their way into a party they knew they weren't invited to. Also, if she got there early enough she would be able to use her game to get into the party with no problem. And that's exactly what she did.

No one was really at the party yet. Everyone was either still downstairs in the lobby, mingling around, or hadn't even gotten to the hotel yet. Lola desperately wanted to go downstairs to get a piece of the action going on in the lobby. But if she left out of the main room, she wouldn't be able to get back in without giving the hostess a valid name on the guest list. And she wasn't about to ruin her chances of making a statement by leaving. So she posted up at a table and ordered a bottle of Chardonnay to help her deal with being alone and whatever else was going to happen that night.

In Lola's mind, all she needed was for Michael to see her tonight. She had on the Vera Wang dress he bought her for Valentine's Day and a pair of 6" Valentino pumps. She wore her hair exactly the way Michael liked it and made sure she had on the Creed perfume that he loved to smell on her. Normally, she would only wear this perfume for him before they were going to make love; but tonight she was pulling out all her guns. She wanted Michael to know she meant business. He was the type that whatever he wanted and no matter what was in his way, he was going to get it. Lola figured that it didn't matter if his wife was here or not; once he saw her, he would get rid of his wife and make a way to give her some of his time and money before the weekend was out.

Outside, Slim met his brother in the huge hotel parking lot that was partially being used for valet parking as well. Slim knew it was going to be hell trying to get his non-connected little brother on the guest list. But with the right calls and a little nose candy added in for the event, he was able to make it happen. Slim knew most of the elite players snorted cocaine and were very discreet with who they shared their personal business with. So being "Texas Slim" had its advantages.

"Damn bruh, man I really appreciate you getting me up in this thing. I feel like I'm finally making the right moves, huh?" Lucky fixed the 1.5 carat diamond cufflinks on his white Ralph Lauren button-up and kept looking at himself being reflected off the shiny surface of his big brother's Silver 760 Beemer, sitting on 21" Forgiato Azioni custom rims.

"Lil nigga, you still got a long way to go. I ain't just wake up and count stacks. I had to grind for the shine and hustle to eat, but yeah, you on your way."

Slim playfully punched his brother on the arm as he led the way to the front entrance of the Four Seasons Hotel. He walked straight through the lobby door without needing to be verified on the guest list. He and his brother looked like a pair of twins out of a GQ magazine as they turned heads. Slim had on a knitted blue sweater and with a white-collar shirt underneath, both made by Hermès. He sported a pair of Dolce & Gabanna shades with a rose-gold trim around the lenses. These weren't the large, tacky stunter shades; these looked more like prescription eyewear that made a bold statement. His navy blue Hermès matching slacks complimented his blue and white ostrich and snakeskin gators. His jewelry didn't say "rap star"; it had more of an executive appeal. He coupled it with a nice rose-gold Breitling watch, a rose-gold pinky ring with blue and white diamonds; two princess-cut earrings in each ear were trimmed in rose-gold with blue diamonds, and a small rose-gold chain with an aqua blue Jesus piece similar to the design Kanye West made famous. Texas Slim matched from his shoes to his ice. He couldn't let some famous ball players show him out; not in his city, not today, tomorrow, next week, or next year.

"Damn bruh, look at these niggas. Is that Carmelo Anthony over there? Aaay Melo!" The nigga Drill was gone trip when Lucky told him about this.

"Listen Luck, chill bro. Don't act star-struck. Just blend in. Shit, you look like you might play in the D-League yourself so stop dick-riding and enjoy yourself. Shit, if you're lucky like your name you might fuck her tonight," Slim said, pointing over in Taz and Veronica's direction as they headed their way.

When Lucky noticed the woman his brother was pointing at, he couldn't have been more elated. Not only had he taken out his "snatch-out" grill, but he was sporting his pearly white smile with a peppermint toothpick in his mouth. He knew tonight he was about to rub shoulders with ballers. And even though he didn't have the type of money his brother had, he sure knew how to floss and look the part. Lucky had on a "now and later" pink V-neck Polo sweater with a white Ralph Lauren button-up. It was a cool Texas night but he still wasn't about to have his balls cooped up in some pants. So he killed the game with his plaid multi-colored polo shorts. Not to be outdone by big bruh, he had on the low-cut Polo socks with the pink jockey symbol and all-white Polo skippers. He'd also borrowed his brother's exclusive pink, blue and yellow Breitling watch coupled with his own four-row yellow diamond bracelet and a matching yellow and orange iced-out chain sporting the Houston Rockets trademark as an emblem. His brother had told him he looked like a fucking drug dealer/rapper right out of a Young Dro video. But Lucky never listened —never.

* * * * * * * * *

"I tell your lil ass what, let them muthafucking cops come to my door talking about you broke in somebody house and I'ma beat the shit out of your bitch-ass." Shelly was in the kitchen smoking a joint while she bagged up one hundred dollar slabs to distribute in the trap. Erin Walters, aka Lucky, had been accused of breaking in several homes in the neighborhood and that was all Shelly needed was extra heat brought to her door. Shit,

Shelly Walters, also known as "Big Shells," sold more dope than a little bit. Her husband, Eric Walters, Sr. aka Rambo was the father of Lucky and his brother Eric Jr. aka Slim, who was a known jack-boy. Rambo hated hustling. He figured it took too much time and attention. He'd rather rob niggas for their money and dope; let Shells get the free dope and profit off of it since she was the dope dealer, not him.

After hooking up with his boy, Juice, he decided he needed to graduate from taking bricks to running up inside of banks. After a failed bank robbery in which he killed two guards and one innocent civilian, he ended up not only being shot twice in the back and paralyzed from the neck down by an off-duty officer depositing his check, but Rambo got life in the infamous federal penitentiary in Colorado. At that point it was all on Shells to take care of two kids and one of them was bad as fuck: Lucky. Shelly wasn't a little lady. She stood at 5'9" and weighed a little bit over 185 pounds. She wore different wigs to hide the fact that she had cancer, but she dressed her ass off.

"Mama, it wasn't me. I swear, I ain't did nothing. You don't never believe me. You always go against me," Lucky whined.

Just when Shelly started to feel sorry for him she heard a knock at the door that changed their lives forever. "Oh shit, that's the goddamn laws. Eric, baby, light some incense." As Eric rushed to the kitchen to light the incense sticks they bought from the Chinese dollar store, lil Erin started crying. "Shut yo' ass up, nigga. Fuck!" Shells took all the dope off the table which totaled just a little over six ounces and threw everything in her black make-up bag. "Um, who is it...ah...I mean, hold on!" she called out. She knew her front screen door was locked due to the jack-boys in the hood, but she also knew the police wouldn't wait long before they tried to get up in there. The police department had been on Shells for years; ever since Rambo was incarcerated and couldn't wait for her to fuck up. Word was that one of the security guards had been the mayor's nephew.

"Rambo smoked the wrong cracker that day," was all people kept saying.

It didn't help that Shells was a shit-starter, a home wrecker and beat bitches up because those hoes were the first to call Crime Stoppers and drop dimes about people selling dope.

"Ma'am, open up the door. We got a call about a young man breaking into some houses."

The white rookie officer was new to this area but was taking no chances. He knew a situation could turn hostile at any moment so he kept his service revolver low while his partner knocked on the door with his flashlight.

"Sims, fuck it! It's too hot to be out here all day about a fucking bastard stealing in his own community. Plus, I don't feel like doing paperwork right before my shift ends."

Rodriguez had a few years under his belt and knew this was the basic "kid doing dumb shit" type of case. He'd rather be in his patrol car with the A/C on. "Don't you smell that? I smell marijuana and that's enough probable cause to at least search the premises. Plus, I know that we have had several complaints about the ongoing traffic at this address."

As Shelly flushed what she could her toilet began to stop up. "Fuck!" She cursed and grabbed the plunger.

Lucky walked to the front screen door, crying. "Hey there little fella, are you the one breaking into old folks homes?" Rodriguez asked. Lucky shook his head, no, and continued crying. "Open the door; we won't hurt you, okay? Where's your mother?"

As Shelly continued to plunge and flush she thought she heard officers in her house. Not even thinking about the two and a half ounces still floating in the toilet, she ran to the living room. Shelly heard, "That's right, unlock the top lock…" as she reached the living room. When she reached the front door she could have strangled Lucky. "Nooo…" Shelly whispered loudly as she remembered the dope and ran back into the bathroom as the police burst inside the house with the turn of a lock. As she reached inside the toilet to grab the remaining dope, trying to conceal and hide it, the two officers rushed into the bathroom

"She's got a gun!" Sims yelled as he fired his service revolver twice, catching Shells in her left eye and stomach.

Although Shelly survived after several surgeries, she was charged with possession with intent to distribute narcotics, child endangerment, resisting arrest and possession of a .32 and Tech 9 with scratched off serial numbers. She knew the gun wasn't hers and after thinking awhile she knew it wasn't Rambo's. The police clearly planted it. Whatever the case, it was an open and shut dope and pistol "trigger locked" federal case. Shelly was sentenced to 27 years in a women's federal penitentiary. Slim and Lucky were sent to live with her sister, Rita, who was also a dope girl but more on the low.

To this day Slim called his little brother Lucky because he used to say, "Nigga, if momma didn't go to jail or get shot or never caught that case, she would have beat the shit out of your dumb ass for opening the door. You lucky she 'locked up.'"

And that was true. Shells hated her son because of his mistake as a child. She hadn't answered one letter he'd written to her over twelve years; any money he sent her she'd send it back; and she burned any picture he sent her of himself. When Lucky went to prison she wished the worse for him. She prayed he got raped, sliced up, or just killed himself. As for Slim, he was her heart and soul; her first, her everything. But anytime he brought up Lucky's name she would say, "Who? He still alive? I don't know him. Lucky who?" So Slim quit trying a long time ago. Years later Shelly would die of cancer, still hating her son.

* * * * * * * * *

As Taz and Veronica got within ten feet of the men, Taz said, "Oh hell nawl. I know this ain't the same fool from earlier at the airport."

Veronica rolled her neck and said, "Who?" as they got closer.

Taz said, "Him," and pointed at Lucky as she walked right past him and his brother.

"Yeah, bitch. Look at me now. Yeah, spin off your ancient-ass spinner. Big Luck dawg up in here, shawty."

Veronica stood there with her hand on her hip and looked Slim up and down. "Would someone please tell me what's going on and who is this loud-ass nigga? Young Dro or something with that loud-ass pink on? Nigga, this ain't South Beach!"

Lucky had heard enough. He had been clowned twice in one day; first his boy and now by the same flock of hoes from the airport.

"Wait! Hold on Veronica, this is my little brother, Lucky. And you look nice, too," he said sarcastically, defending his brother.

"I'm just saying Slim, my girl..." But Taz interrupted Veronica.

"You know what? I'm sorry, what is it, Lucky, Lookey, Lucey or whatever. I'm out," and Taz quickly walked away.

Veronica walked quickly away as well and tried to catch up with Taz, who was on her cell phone. When she caught up with her she overheard part of her conversation.

"Darryl I know. Just please come and get me. I'll be waiting out front." Taz looked at Veronica. "I don't know what type of shit you on now but I'm out!"

Veronica spoke up. "Wait a minute, will you tell me what's going on first? Damn!"

Taz looked at Veronica and realized it was Lola who saw those dudes at the airport and not Veronica. "I'm sorry. It's a long story that happened at the airport earlier. Lola was there but I'm out of here." Shit was about to pop off.

Inside the hotel all Lola could think about was how that bitch-ass wife of Michael's was show-boating for all his friends and all the spectators like she was the shit, when all was said and done she was nothing more than a worthless piece of trash in Lola's eyes. Lola envied the life she had. She had everything Lola ever dreamed of. Michael's wife, Vanessa, was what most men would consider flawless. She was tall like a model and reminded you of a beautiful Naomi Campbell type with the body of Serena Williams, who was also one of her closest friends. She had long, thick curly hair similar to Tracee Ellis Ross and never wore any heavy makeup. Her skin was a golden, dark bronze color almost like Ethiopian coloring. She definitely fit the look that athletes wanted on their arm. His wife was not just a trophy wife; she was an all-around business woman and a damn good one at that.

All of Michael's affairs were run by his wife in one way or another. If he wrote a book, her company published it. If he made an appearance her management team got a percentage. Even when he was in the NBA, her stepfather was his agent and responsible for the multi-million dollar contracts he received. No matter what, Vanessa always got a piece of the pie and that's exactly how she intended to keep it. Vanessa didn't need Michael and since they were no longer in love with each other, Lola figured Vanessa must have been getting great pleasure out of making Michael's life a living hell. Lola couldn't figure out why, but she knew there was more to this marriage than Michael would ever let her know. She wondered if there was a side to Michael she'd never seen and if she was playing with fire by trying to come between the two. This was a risk Lola was willing to take. She had not come all the way to Houston to leave empty-handed. And she damn sure wasn't going to let that nothing-ass Vanessa stand in the way of her money bag. Lola was playing for keeps and nothing was going to stand in her way.

CHAPTER 25

"Yeah nigga, don't worry about that. It'll be here tonight. By the time we head back upstate we definitely gonna be clean out," Rain said calmly while on the phone with his country boys from Dallas who were in town. Rain was Darryl's right-hand man and anyone who was familiar with their circle knew Darryl was the boss. Darryl didn't talk on the phone unless in codes and on a throw-away, do transactions, or any of the above. He was the kingpin. He never touched or said anything which involved his work. Darryl and his crew gave the appearance of being in Houston and just having a good time at the All-Star game. However, that was not the case. The All-Star game was the perfect setup for them to meet up with all their clients in one weekend and make a huge come up. With the dope coming in right next door from Mexico, their plan was brilliant. Darryl planned to go home with at least 3.5 million dollars in cold, hard cash.

They were there to work. They had workers setup on each end of Houston, ready to accommodate their clientele. They had people who had driven in from everywhere: Atlanta, Memphis, New Orleans, Baton Rouge, Dallas, Phoenix and even Miami. Darryl had a new connect in Mexico he wanted to try. So for this first go round, if the niggas wanted the dope, he was making them come and get it themselves. If all went well, this connect was going to take Darryl out of the game sooner than he expected.

They picked Houston to score big because it was where the new connect wanted to meet, and it was also a central meeting point for everyone. Instead of all his clients having to make that long drive to New York, he figured he could get them all in the same place; and at the same time he could eliminate having to do any of the work and be able to sit back and count all of the profit —almost four million dollars in drug money. Darryl loved that idea. He had been turned onto his new connect by this old head out of Phoenix named Kilo. Darryl met Kilo while he was in the fed pen serving a five-year bid for gun charges. Kilo promised Darryl that when he got out and if Darryl was still alive and on his feet, he would hook Darryl up for a small fee of a quarter million dollars. Darryl was willing and ready to get the deal going and knew a quarter million dollars was nothing compared to the dough he would be bringing in once everything was set up. This connect was responsible for setting a lot of niggas straight. He knew the game very well and also had several connects in place to make transactions go as smoothly as possible. From what Darryl had heard, it seemed as if this connect had dope coming in from all over. With a connect like this, and a right-hand man like Rain, Darryl planned to take over the South without having to leave his penthouse in Brooklyn.

Rain was the type who believed there were too many Chiefs and not enough Indians. He loved playing his position as right-hand man. Loyalty was a huge part of his upbringing. Rain came from a family of pimps, hustlers, drug dealers, prostitutes and strippers. The game was in his bloodline and he wasn't trying to shake it anytime soon. Rain reminded you of Money Making Mitch from the movie "Paid in Full." He was all about his business and didn't have to be "the man" to prove anything. He was content with his position and knew that as long as he played it well his position with the team was secure.

While everyone else in Houston was partying, Rain and Darryl were getting their paper up. But his phone was blowing up. After hitting ignore three times already, Darryl finally answered. "Yeah baby girl, what's up?"

"Hello, hello, Darryl? Damn, I been trying to call you for about an hour. When you see this number you need to learn to answer the fucking phone!"

"Shit, my bad, shawty. Nigga out here sliding and making moves."

"Yeah, whatever nigga. I know you're probably out having fun but I'm in a real uncomfortable situation and I need you to pick me up from this party downtown at the Four Seasons," Taz said.

"Baby, I already told you, tonight is an extremely busy night for me. Can you catch a cab? You should have more than enough money," Darryl said.

"Darryl, I know; but just please come and get me. I'll be waiting out front." Darryl hesitantly agreed and hung up the phone. He instructed Rain to head downtown.

"Man, what the fuck we going into the middle of downtown for? We riding dirty as a muthafucka and you want to go into downtown Houston traffic? Are you crazy, nigga?" said Rain.

"I know man, but shawty is in a fucked up situation and need me to scoop her and take her back to the hotel."

"Shawty, who the fuck is shawty?" snapped Rain.

"You know, Taz, lil mama from earlier, the Cheesecake Factory and the mall," said Darryl.

"Yo', you better be fucking her at the end of tonight cause you bugging son, real talk. Now how do I get to the Four Seasons?" Rain asked.

Darryl knew he really didn't have an option but to pick up Taz from the hotel, especially considering he had already invested quite a bit in her. He knew a woman of Taz's caliber would never speak to him again and keep every dime he'd given to her in that package if he didn't rescue her from harm's way. So Darryl knew he had to pick his new lil mama up immediately. As thick and as fine as Taz was, Darryl knew picking her up in combination with the shopping and the package he'd left her at the front desk, he was definitely getting into them draws. All he could imagine was Taz's butt, ass-naked with a slim waistline and a fat ass. He imagined her pussy shaved with a tattoo of a butterfly in between her pussy and thigh. Just thinking about Taz bent over the edge of his marble bathroom sink in his penthouse in New York had Darryl's dick rock hard. He could not only tell she was going to be a good fuck, but the way that bitch was shaped he could tell she probably knew how to shake that ass, too. He wanted her to be his own private little dancer. He was more than willing to throw some ones onto her fine ass. The way Taz's ass jiggled when she walked, he couldn't wait to slap some Ben Franklins on her ass.

"Nigga, what the fuck is wrong with you? Yo', I been calling your name for the last three fucking minutes, B," Rain yelled. Darryl looked down and saw his dick was hard as shit from daydreaming the past 20 minutes about fucking Taz. "Nigga, we here. Wake your bitch-ass up," Rain joked with Darryl. Darryl looked up to see them pulling up in front of the lobby of the Four Seasons Hotel. It was packed as hell. "Damn, Darryl. Looks like your new bitch, Taz, on that high-class shit. She damn sure picked the party that all of the bosses are at. Judging from these whips out here these niggas at this party are on. We need to find out who holding," Rain said as he observed everything.

"Nigga, we holding. What the fuck you mean we need to find out who holding? I can guarantee our pockets are more flooded than any nigga out here. And if they ain't, nigga after this weekend they will be. Taz ain't thinking 'bout these niggas. You see she called a real nigga to pick her ass up. She know who got that cake," Darryl laughed.

Inside the hotel, Taz sat in a chair in the lobby wondering where the fuck Darryl was. She was constantly being tormented by Lucky. He kept walking past her saying slick-ass comments like, "She need some dick. Bitch got the nerve to be acting like she all that. Give a nigga some of that ass, girl. I got something for you bitch, a fat-ass dick for that smart-ass mouth of yours." As bad as Taz wanted to go in on Lucky's young, broke ass, she knew the Four Seasons Hotel wasn't the time or place. Taz looked around repeatedly for Veronica. But as nasty as she had been to Veronica she didn't expect her to come anywhere near her. She was probably headed back to the hotel or somewhere all up in Slim's face Taz was thinking to herself. So she just sat there, waiting until she would get that phone call from Darryl.

On the other hand, Slim was blowing Lucky's cellphone up, but the reception in the lobby was so bad he wasn't able to get through. "What the fuck happened between your girl and my brother that's got everybody so shook?" Slim snapped at Veronica.

"First off nigga, don't raise your fucking voice at me. I don't fucking know. I was trying to ask Taz but she was too busy being a bitch to answer my question. I'm just as lost as you are. She mentioned Lola was there. Shit, let me call her to see what the fuck was going on," Veronica said.

"Shit, knowing my little brother, he probably fucked her and don't want nothing else to do with her ass. So she salty about that shit," Slim said.

Veronica looked at Slim and said sarcastically, "Nigga, are you out of your muthafucking mind? I don't roll with duck-ass bitches. Your little "now and later" pink-wearing, broke-ass brother wouldn't stand a fucking chance with Taz. He's not a muthafucking factor, and as a matter of fact, neither are you, nigga. You have been dismissed so get the fuck outta my face!" Veronica told Slim in her nastiest voice ever while casually putting on another coat of her princess-cut diamond lip gloss just to piss him off.

"Aight then, have it your way, baby. But you better be careful how you talk to niggas down here in Texas, bitch cause any other nigga would have slapped the taste out of your pretty-ass mouth," laughed Slim as he walked off like the shit didn't faze him. Then he goes off to look for Lucky. "Shouldn't of brought this retarded nigga wit me."

Lola heard her phone ping and looked at the screen. There was a text message which read, *"It's an emergency. Please pick up phone."* It was from Veronica. Lola called her. "What's up? I'm at a party."

"I'm at the Four Seasons Hotel with Taz and some shit just popped off. I need to know what happened earlier at the airport with some young niggas," Veronica said.

Lola immediately smiled. "Damn Karma came around quick as a muthafucka. I hope that nigga saw that smart-mouth bitch and slapped the shit outta her ass," Lola said as she stepped into the bathroom to talk to Veronica.

"Hello, hello. Hold up, let me step outside. This reception is fucked up," Veronica said as she walked into a stairwell leading to the outside of the Four Seasons. She opened the door and stepped outside.

"What's going on?" asked Lola.

"Girl, that's what the fuck I'm trying to find out. What the fuck happened at the airport with some broke-ass niggas? One named Lucky," asked Veronica.

"Oh, you talking 'bout at baggage claim. Shit, I don't know the niggas' names, but some nigga was talking reckless to Taz so of course her and her smart-ass mouth went in on him. Don't tell me y'all ran back into those niggas?"

"Girl, hell yes. I met this nigga named Slim at the hotel earlier and come to find out Slim is the nigga Lucky's brother," Veronica told her. "So when we all linked up all hell broke loose. I don't even know where the bitch is right now. She took off and called the nigga Darryl to come and pick her up. I'm sitting here like, what the fuck?" As Veronica stood near a stinking-ass dumpster on the side of the hotel, all she could think about was if she should take her ass home or go back into the party and enjoy the rest of her night. She decided to stick around. Even though she didn't know Taz that well, she wasn't leaving until she knew one hundred percent that Taz was straight.

"Baby girl, I wish I could help you but I'm actually all the way on the other side of town at a party hosted by Zach Randolph and Master P. If you need me just text me back. Girl, Webbie is staring down my throat. I gotta go," Lola lied as she practically hung up on Veronica. The last thing on Lola's mind was some stupid-ass fight between Veronica and Taz. She was waiting on her man to walk in, and by the look of the clock that should be at any moment. Lola knew Michael always did a walkthrough at all of his events to make sure everything was straight before they started allowing too many guests in. She knew he was definitely on his way.

Veronica looked at her phone and rolled her eyes. "Bitch!" she said as she looked at the blank screen and put the phone in her purse. She looked up just in time to see Darryl's aqua blue Bentley GT circling around the parking lot, apparently looking for Taz. She started making her way around the side of the building to the parking lot in hopes of flagging Darryl down. As Veronica raced towards the driver's window of Darryl's car, Rain tried to swerve around her, not initially knowing who she was. But by the looks of things this girl was headed straight for the driver's window.

"Look at this thirsty bitch here. Out of all the niggas out here, this bitch chooses to run her dark ass up to my car. I don't even like dark-skinned bitches. Shit, she do got a nice lil ass on her though," Darryl said.

As Rain looked closely at the girl running up to the car, he burst out laughing. He noticed the girl was Veronica. "Nigga, that's Veronica, one of the shawty's from earlier. Nigga you're a fucking beast when it comes to dogging these hoes." They both laughed. Rain slowed down the car so that Veronica could walk up to it.

"Damn nigga, what the fuck is wrong with you? I know you saw me trying to flag your ass down." Then she sees Rain is the driver and said, "Hey Rain…boo. You gone have a bitch musty as hell fucking around with you." Veronica was paranoid, looking around to make sure Slim was nowhere in sight.

"Shit, my bad, shawty," Darryl said, leaning forward and looking at her. "I didn't know who the fuck you was and the last thing I wanted was for Taz to roll up on me while I'm talking to another shawty. I can tell she don't play that shit. And speaking of Taz, where the fuck she at? I been calling her phone for about ten minutes and its going straight to voicemail. And if you're here why did she need me to pick her up?"

"Shit Darryl, she ended up seeing some niggas in there that she had a run-in with a while back and she wasn't feeling the situation, so she got the fuck out of dodge. Why she called you? I don't know cause I would have taken her back to her room. Shit, maybe she just wanted an excuse to see you tonight," Veronica said sarcastically while giving Darryl a look that gave him high hopes that Taz might want to fuck him tonight.

But as Veronica looked around again, she saw Slim and Lucky exit from a side door of the hotel, heading towards the parking lot. She knew in order to keep the heat off her and to keep her from looking like a groupie to Rain, she was going to have to choose sides quickly. She knew if she continued to fuck with Slim it probably meant Taz was not going to fuck with her anymore and she definitely did not want that. She decided it was more beneficial for her to point out who the men were before Lucky and his big-ass mouth put her on blast. So she pulled a quick move.

"Shit, there go the nigga right there. The short, country-ass muthafucka walking next to Slim...I mean the tall dude," she corrected herself, realizing she had already let Slim's name slip out of her mouth. She didn't let them see her sweat. Slim was in fact skinny so she figured they would just think she used the name "Slim" to describe the dude.

"Yo', why the fuck was Taz even wasting energy on a bird-brain, country-ass nigga like that? The nigga looks mad wack," Darryl said with a confused look on his face.

Veronica wasn't interested in shit Darryl was saying at that point. She couldn't help but notice that Lucky and Slim had suddenly changed course and were walking closer and closer towards the Bentley. She knew she had been spotted.

* * * * * * * * *

"T'ma take care of you baby. You ain't never gonna have to worry about nothing," said Slim to Myesha. After Slim found out Myesha was pregnant he wanted to give her the world. Slim was a made nigga. Not only did his father, Rambo, leave him a shit load of money before he went to prison for bank robbery, but Slim was known in the hood for getting legal money, too, through professional athletes. He was said to have supplied everything from yellow syrup, double and triple stack ecstasy pills, raw uncut powder, china white aka Bobby Brown, crack aka Whitney Houston, Vicodin, Oxycontin, Percocet and the list goes on. Slim was slated to go into the draft as a first round pick but was eliminate due to an investigation that claimed he received high-end gifts from various resources. He was listed as the number one quarterback in the State of Texas and ranked number three in the nation. The NFL commissioner black-balled him and from there he had only one option: hustling.

After deciding to finish school and get his degree, Slim became a sports agent and somewhat of a financial advisor. He started his own sports agency and opened an accounting firm that did everything from bookkeeping, accounting, financial advising and even provided a concierge service which served all the major cities where athletes traveled to such as New York, Las Vegas, Atlanta, Houston, Los Angeles, New Orleans and anywhere else they wanted to spend their money. Overall, Slim was a pretty well-rounded dude. But once Myesha got ahold of his ass, he turned stingy as hell and didn't look out for family. He would trick-off with hoes, fly bitches to and fro and even splurged in big casinos. But when it came to his family, he only gave them the crumbs he left behind; just enough to keep them satisfied. Myesha had planted so many seeds in Slim's head about why family wasn't shit that he felt no responsibility for them at all. She had Slim completely brainwashed.

"Slim, if you could please just send me a few dollars to get on my feet; things been looking real rough on this end lately and I'm barely making it. I try not to ask you for much, but your auntie is getting old and I need you, son," begged Slim's Aunt Rita. She'd raised him and Lucky when their mother was sent to the federal penitentiary.

"*I got you auntie. Shit, give me a few days to get some money together.*" Slim would say that just to get his aunt off the phone. He never had any real intentions of sending her any money. And if he did, it was never for the amount she asked for. Back in the day, Rita was a dope girl herself. She left the game alone when her sister was sentenced to all those years in prison. She knew prison was no place for her, especially after both Shells and her husband, Rambo, were ordered to spend damn near the rest of their lives in prison. She wasn't having that shit.

Rita and the rest of the family didn't understand why Slim acted the way he did. But everyone was always too scared to confront him or say something to him about it because they all knew where it stemmed from; that coldhearted bitch Myesha. Slim pretty much shitted on everybody except for his trick-ass baby-momma, Myesha. She was a fly-bitch, one of those bitches who had so much game because she was practically raised by pimps and hoes. Myesha's momma would tell her every day she came home from school or after a date with Slim with all kinds of advice such as "*I ain't raising no broke-ass bitches. I want you at every muthafucking game, cheering that ballplayer nigga on. As fine as you is I don't ever want you broke a day in your life. I want you to stay on that nigga like white on rice. He's going to the pros, girl. Listen to ya momma, baby. He's gonna be the nigga with a hell of a lot of money that can take care of you your entire life. And I want you to have a baby by that nigga. That way, if he ever leave your ass, you still gone get paid, regardless. They giving over twenty grand a month to bitches these days. Look at Puff Daddy, or is it Ruff Puffy, Diddy or whatever the hell his name is, baby-mommas. Basically what I'm saying is, fuck his momma, fuck his daddy, fuck everybody. Make it so it's all about you and let the rest fend for they damn selves.*"

Nobody could figure out why Myesha had such a strong-ass hold over Slim. She would leave him then come back and then leave him again. She'd even go fuck one of his homeboys and then come back again, spend his money and play with his head by telling him she wanted a family then leave him again. She didn't want him but she damn sure wasn't about to let any other *bitch have him. She knew Slim was a good nigga, but Slim couldn't give Myesha what she wanted which was a nigga in the limelight. She was an "attention whore" who wanted to be seen every chance she got. She wanted to be a baller's wife and not the wife of an average Joe-ass nigga. Although Slim's money was long, in fact longer than some ballplayers, Myesha didn't want that. She wanted fame. And not only was she a scandalous bitch with a pretty face and bad-ass body, she was a home wrecker.*

Back when Myesha was pregnant and thought Slim was going to the pros, she made a vow to herself that she was going to do what her momma taught her. Slim wasn't going to be one of those athletes who went broke due to taking care of their entire family and their nothing-ass niggas from the hood. Myesha drew a big line between Slim and his family. She was determined to be the head-bitch-in-charge. She wanted to be the only bitch getting that money. His momma was now dead, his father was still locked up and his little brother was a nothing-ass hood rat. She figured the rest of his family didn't matter. She and his son, Baby Slim, would be his family and fuck the rest of them. She was so cold that when Slim's momma died of cancer in prison, she convinced him to buy a cheap casket. "What she need an expensive casket for? She dead."

* * * * * * * * *

As Veronica stood at the window of the Bentley she knew the situation was about to get ugly.

"Damn baby, this who you fuck wit? You's a thot, huh?" Texas Slim said loudly from more than three feet away.

"Bitch-ass nigga, I ain't no thot, your baby, lil ma or none of that lame-ass shit. Why the fuck you stalking me?" Veronica asked as she looked from Rain to Slim to Darryl.

Rain, being the boss that he was, definitely wasn't about to put his money and life in jeopardy for this "basic-ass bitch" he thought to himself. "Yo' ma, fallback and let me do the talking. Matter of fact, get yo' dumb-ass in the car," Rain said, getting out and opening the Bentley's door.

"Bruh, look at these lame duck-ass niggas trying to stunt on us. Pussy-ass nigga, get yo' punk-ass back in that car before I slang this drakostick and spray up that rented-ass Bentley, fuck nigga." Lucky was talking big shit to Rain with his hand underneath his Polo shirt like he was strapped, but he wasn't. He was doing what you called "pump-faking," a term used meaning he was bluffing.

Veronica, who was half-way in the car, turned around and ran towards Lucky, swinging and screaming, "I'm tired of yo' goddamned mouth, nigga!"

Lucky side-stepped Veronica and caught her with two sharp jabs to the side of her head, causing her to become dizzy and punch-drunk.

At that moment, Taz came out of the hotel looking for Darryl and saw the commotion. She ran towards them, highly pissed off that she just witnessed Lucky "dog walk" her girl. Without thinking twice, Taz slaps Lucky from the back and yelled, "Bitch-ass, nigga!"

Lucky, who was quick and had fight game, turned around and started choking the shit out of Taz. "Bitch! You crazy, shawty. You wanted this. You just can't stay in your place!"

Slim grabs Lucky by the shoulder, trying to calm him down and to get him to let Taz loose. "Bruh, let her go. Let's bounce, mane."

Lucky, not knowing it was Slim who had grabbed him, instinctively turned around and gave Slim an uppercut that dazed him.

By that time, Rain had already heard, seen and had enough. He reacted quickly and yanked out the two twin .40 Cal. sticks and pointed them at Slim and Lucky. "You cornball-ass niggas on some joke-ass shit? Lay the fuck down, son."

Darryl had gotten out of the car and was helping Taz up while mugging Lucky. Everything was happening so quickly; too quickly. It seemed as if there was total chaos in the parking lot. There were so many onlookers that Darryl was sure 5-0 was on the way. As he helped Taz to her feet, he yelled at Rain, "If any one of them country-ass niggas move let 'em know we 'bout that "stick-talk," as he helped a pissed off Taz into the backseat of the Bentley. But Taz just couldn't shut the fuck up.

"Broke-asses on the ground, looking like some bitches. You see this whip? This says money. Something yo' broke asses ain't never had!" This childish back and forth shit between Taz and Lucky erupted again causing Lucky to reach into his pocket.

* * * * * * * * *

"Lavern Jordan, do you want to share with the class what you and Jamichael are talking about?" Their ninth grade math teacher, Mrs. Cantrell, had been trying to prepare her students for a test, but it was always Lavern "Rain" Jordan who just couldn't stop being the center of attention.

"Yeah, I was just telling my man that them shits you got on your feet are mad old. You must have gotten them from Harriet Tubman."

The class burst out in an uproar of laughter while the white teacher's face turned beet red. "Get out! Get out! Go to the principal's office now!"

"Yeah, yeah, yeah. Save the drama for yo' mama," Rain said. As he walked to the principal's office he stopped in the boy's bathroom. It smelled just like a high school boy's bathroom should smell, like straight piss. As he stood, taking a piss, he sang his favorite anthem by his favorite rapper. "It

was all a dream, I used to read…" He was stopped midsentence by the feel of cold iron being pushed directly into the center of his back.

"Bitch, either you holding out on my paper or you're smoking my shit. Now which excuse are you going to die for today?"

Rain knew that voice. It was Hotshot, a bully from his projects who Rain was moving a little weed and crack for just to help his moms out and stay fresh. "Look yo', first of all, take that burner up out of my back unless you gone squeeze. And second of all…"

At that moment the principal—who had received an urgent message that someone who didn't attend the school was on the premises—walked into the bathroom. "Young men, what the hell is going on?"

Although Rain was known as a troublemaker, he was happy Mr. Brent saved the day. He was a white guy who stood 6'4" with a very slim build and favored Jim Carrey. He didn't like Rain because he knew he was selling the other kids drugs. One of the kids was his own daughter who they said Rain was fucking the shit out of. Mr. Brent had him now. "Man, am I happy to see you "fire marshal Bill," joked Rain.

Hotshot felt as if he was trapped so he turned and started walking toward the restroom's door. With his gun still drawn he said, "Move old man." Mr. Brent didn't move as quickly as Hotshot wanted him to. BOOM! BOOM! BOOM! BOOM! BOOM! Hotshot fed the principal five shots and darted out the bathroom, but not before aiming at Rain. "Bye-bye, bitch." Click-click-click. The gun was either empty or jammed. Hotshot threw it at Rain and ran. To this day, Rain never knew why the gun didn't shoot, but he did know he was fucked.

The principal made a slow, but complete, recovery following surgery and the loss of a kidney. He told authorities he knew who shot him and would never forget his face. He identified the shooter, telling the detectives, "It was Lavern Jordan." He also told them he caught Rain in the boy's bathroom, raping his daughter and he tried to save his only child. "I begged him to stop," he said, "but he pointed the gun at me and laughed. I felt so helpless with my precious little girl screaming, 'help me daddy' and this monster ripping her insides up. I told him I could get him help and he pointed the gun at me and told me not even God could help him. Then all I remembered was a loud boom!" Rain's teacher even testified that Rain had a bulge under his shirt during class and she knew it was a gun because he had told several students it was a gun. He couldn't believe his teacher and principal had lied on him.

Hotshot ended up going to Seattle with his brother, never to be heard from again. Rain was sent to a New York reformatory school for boys until the age of 18 and then to Riker's Island to complete his adult sentence until the age of 21. At 15, reformatory school in New York for any black boy was hell. The first day would prove to be a taste of hell's kitchen for Rain. "Bend over and spread 'em gentlemen; and cough two times," the heavyset, prejudiced white deputy staff member told the teenagers who were in the R and R stage of incarceration. Rain, who had never been locked up a day in his life, wasn't with this fag-ass procedure.

"Hey fat ass, why don't you bend over and spread 'em."

The other boys dared not laugh. They were second and third time offenders and knew the consequences to come for that remark. "What the fuck did you say to me, nigger boy?" the white staff member replied as he walked over and shoved a finger into Rain's chest.

Rain, who thought everything was a joke, laughed. But Sergeant Sweeney walked into the shower area to help speed up the intake process asked, "What's this nigger's problem, Tom?" Sweeney was a redneck and had a nightstick in his hand.

"This damn nigger-boy has a big mouth. I think he wants to be in charge."

Sergeant Sweeney chuckled and gave a cold stare to the other young men, signaling it was time for them to face the wall. Then Sweeney walked over to Rain and shoved the nightstick into his stomach. When Rain tried to get *aggressive, the Sergeant pulled back and rammed the stick so hard into Rain's midsection that he shit on himself. "Goddamned nigger done shit! Would you look at that, Tom? Look like this nigger's gonna get his breakfast after all."*

Tom proceeded to punch Rain with closed fists until Rain put up no struggle. Then he pushed Rain's face into his own feces. "Now eat, nigger, and I mean smack like it's ya mammie's chicken, ya hear?"

After Rain finished to their satisfaction, Sergeant Sweeney slammed Rain's face into the marble floor until he almost couldn't breathe and said, "You gone learn boy that we break the toughest niggers in New York City, especially little nigger rapists who rape our daughters." What Rain didn't know was that his former principal personally wrote the warden and asked for harsh punishment for Rain after he found out his daughter was pregnant with Rain's child.

His daughter told him she loved Rain and threatened to tell the truth. So he slipped 15 sleeping pills into her orange juice one morning at breakfast. By the time his daughter realized the juice tasted funny, she had taken two large gulps of it. It was too late. She started feeling very tired and went back to her bedroom—which was painted yellow and pink and covered with old Barbie doll and Justin Timberlake posters—and lay back down. She thought she was feeling so tired because of the pregnancy. Unfortunately, that was her last thought because Sarah Brent and her baby died in her sleep at the tender age of 15. The death happened right before Rain was sentenced and the media blew it up as a rape victim committing suicide because of how embarrassed and traumatized she was. This made the white communities around New York furious and that's what turned Rain's life.

"Now that you've had your breakfast, nigger, here's your drink." Both staff members pulled down their workpants and held their little pink penises while pissing all over Rain. "Golden shower, nigga; real porno shit."

Rain lay on the cold shower floor, plotting revenge and crying. But this was only the beginning for young Rain. Tears from the angels were definitely falling tonight.

CHAPTER 26

As the DJ blasted Philthy Phil's latest single "I'm Gangsta," Michael walked through the party like he owned the world. As he mumbled the words to the single, *"I'm gangsta, I'm gangsta, you know it, you know it,"* he bobbed his head and let the Grey Goose and weed in his system work their magic. "Shit, ain't no need to play in the league when I still got all this money to blow. I could do this shit every day for the rest of my life," he said to himself. As he maneuvered his way to his NBA partners, he noticed they were in a circle being entertained by a familiar voice.

"Man, she's drunk." "Shawty got a nice lil ass." "Mane, I'd love to hit that." All these comments were being said as Michael walked up. More concerned with his reputation he moved in quickly. "What the fuck?" he said.

Lola stood there looking drunk, but sexy, as she shook her ass to the latest Philthy Phil song over the speakers, *"This my sh..."* Michael quickly grabbed her by the hair. "Muthafuc..." But before Lola could say anything else, Michael placed his fingers on the back of her neck. "Dang baby, you trippin'..." was all Lola could say, sounding like a little kid.

"Now listen bitch, and you listen good. It's over! O-V-E-R!" He signaled for security and they came quickly and escorted a drunken Lola out the party.

"Bitch!" And she started kicking, biting and scratching at the two security guards. "Bitch, it ain't over! It ain't over cause I'm keeping this baby, bitch!"

Michael never heard her last words. He was too busy trying to make sure his wife wasn't around. What he didn't know was that his wife was upstairs in a presidential suite getting her freak on with an ex-76er that now played in the Big 3 League. Not only was she coked up, but she was getting run by him and his partner.

As Lola was shoved out the hotel into the cold air she was furious. "Huh, muthafucka want to play?" she said out loud under her breath to no one in particular. "Okay, I ain't gone trip. Don't even trip Lola. I got you, nigga. Yeah, I got yo' ass." She tried to scan the crowd for a new baller she could get back into the party with when she heard a commotion toward the side of the building. She thought she heard Taz's voice, but she brushed it off as nothing and continued her search, stumbling around, drunk and all.

* * * * * * * * *

As Lucky lay on the ground he knew he was tired of Taz stunting on him and calling him broke. That's when he reached into the pocket of his Polo pants to pull out his bankroll.

"You reaching, son?" was all Rain said as he let off two shots that missed Lucky. Slim, being the protector and big brother, couldn't stand back and play the sucka role any longer, not in his own city.

"Nigga, fuck you!" Slim said and stood up and rushed Rain. Rain raised his second pistol and fired both guns rapidly into Slim's chest.

"Come on, let's get out of here, son. Let's bounce!" Darryl shouted at Rain.

As the Bentley screeched out of the parking lot, Slim lay shaking on the ground. Lucky was trying to hold his brother.

"Damn nigga," Slim said, "I can't breathe. Take this vest off me, bruh." Lucky proceeded to take the vest off Slim and he could see that two bullets caught him outside his vest and he was losing blood fast.

"Damn bro, I can't just leave you but I got warrants, too, fuck!" Lucky could hear sirens in the background and knew if he was caught at the scene it wouldn't be pretty. He had warrants out of Dallas for a dumb-ass jewelry store heist where he dropped his cellphone as he escaped. He never told Slim because he knew Slim wouldn't be happy about it. Overall, Lucky felt Slim owed him and not the other way around since he let Myesha brainwash him. "I got to go, bruh."

Slim couldn't believe his ears. Here he was with two bullets in his left side and Lucky was about to leave him. Then Lucky did the unthinkable. He reached inside of Slim's pocket and took the car keys.

"Bitch-ass nigga, you really gone leave me here like this? Lucky! Lucky…"

But Lucky had taken off and run to the Beemer and hurriedly got inside. After starting the car, he reached under the passenger seat and grabbed his pistol from where he'd stashed it before going into the hotel. He had no other choice but to steal Slim's car because he'd had one of his bitches drop him off at the hotel so he had no other choice but to take Slim's car. He pulled off and when he got within two feet of Slim, he noticed the parking lot was still in chaos and people were on their phones calling for help for Slim. He figured if he could get Slim in the car with him, he could eliminate himself from being on the scene at all. As he stopped and jumped out the car, he knew he had to act fast. As Lucky tried to get Slim into the car, he felt his body go limp like he had just died; dead-weight was what it felt like. "Damn, fuck it!" So Lucky pushed Slim back to the ground. And just as several police cars pulled up and the officers started making their way from the front to the back of the building, Lucky smashed out the parking lot but realized the car was on empty which forced him to pull into the nearest gas station to get some gas.

* * * * * * * * *

"Let me get a pack of Newports in a box and hurry the fuck up!" Lola said drunk, worried and helpless to the cashier behind the counter of the Chevron. She had caught an Uber that was parked across the street and had stopped because she needed a quick smoke to keep herself from fucking somebody up. By this time Lola's head had started spinning and she could barely stand up or walk straight. She was drunk as hell. As she turned to stagger from the store, she was startled by a very familiar face; a tacky-looking ass nigga. Damn, the nigga was staring dead at her. Lola was confused. She couldn't tell if the nigga was one of Michael's homeboys following her, or if it was some nigga she had kicked to the curb in the past. "What the fuck this psycho-ass nigga looking at?" Lola asked herself. "And where the fuck do I know him from?"

She stepped outside the store, barely walking straight, looking for the Uber driver so she could get a ride back to her hotel to plot her next move on Michael. "Where the fuck this nigga go," Lola said out loud, realizing her Uber driver had left her stranded. The temperature in Houston had dropped dramatically and Lola was stuck outside in the cold. Her face had turned red and she looked down and saw that she had a run in her stockings, bigger than Interstate 285 West, running down both her thighs plus, her cellphone battery was dead. She had to come up with something quick. She turned toward the gas pumps just in time to see that familiar face staring her down while he pumped his last bit of gas.

Maybe she could catch a ride with him. Lola noticed he was looking nervous and hoped he wasn't no fucking serial killer but how the fuck else was she going to get to the hotel?

She was considering packing her shit and heading back to the airport. Then it hit her where she knew the nigga from. Lola's eyes got very big. He was the nigga at the airport Taz had a run-in with earlier. This was perfect timing. She was about to start some shit for sure.

"Hey baby, you just gone stare and not say "hey?" Lola yelled across the gas station lot.

Lucky didn't respond. He couldn't tell where he knew this bitch from. He wasn't sure if she was at the hotel where his brother was just gunned down and saw him, or if she was some random bitch he had fucked previously.

"Naw lil mama, I'm cool. I ain't even on that right now," Lucky replied, wiping the sweat from his forehead.

"You ain't on that? What the fuck you mean you ain't on that, nigga? You must not realize who you talking to. I don't get turned down, I turn niggas down. So like I said..." Lola was interrupted by the Muslim cashier who looked like Abdul from "The Simpsons," the one who ran the Quickie Mart.

He ran outside and started to scream with an Arabian accent, "I don't want to hear this nonsense in front of my store; you are running away all my damn customers. You and your little drunk, high-heel-wearing girlfriend need to get the hell away from my store before I call the cops!"

Lola strutted over and hopped into the passenger seat of the Beemer and Lucky spazzed out on her. "Bitch, get the fuck out my car. You ain't going nowhere with me you drunken mutt!"

Lola looked at Lucky and smirked and laughed and said, "Yes the fuck I am, nigga. I know all about you and what you're hiding from. So if I gotta get out this fucking car, we both going to jail."

Both hesitant and scared, Lucky told the store owner, "You right boss man, we gonna take this little argument elsewhere. No disrespect." Lucky got in the car and smashed away from the gas station. He turned to Lola and snarled, "Now where the fuck you know me from? You better start talking, bitch!"

Lola, scared and drunk, explained everything from the beginning, adding little lies to piss Lucky off and make him feel sorry for her. One thing they had in common was that they wanted Taz dealt with and they wanted that shit done fast. "Yeah, she staying over at the Hotel Derek and her nigga, the one who shot your brother, he holding major weight."

Lucky wasn't even that pissed off about Slim because their bond was broken years ago. He was amped up about this bitch, Taz, and knew she had to be taught a lesson. Although he had a grudge against Slim, he lowered his head and shed a tear, thinking, "Forgive me Lord." Lucky knew he was about to show out.

CHAPTER 27

"Sariyah and McKenzie, get dressed so I can take y'all to your doctor appointments!" yelled Dre as he sat on his plush, white leather sofa that Veronica had purchased with some of her new money. The last two days had been hell for Dre. Even though he was the proud father of two beautiful girls, he'd rather be laid up with his hood rat bitch for the weekend, smoking some Dro, instead of playing babysitter.

"But Dadeee…Dora is not over yet!" yelled the precious-looking McKenzie. Both of the girls favored their mother but acted just like their father.

"Come on McKenzie before daddy gets mad. Hurry up," whined Sariyah as she put on her pink corduroy pants with the matching sweater. They both dressed alike and since Veronica knew Dre was lazy, she made sure she had their play clothing and school clothing all laid out just in case any sudden event popped up.

Dre was what you called an "alright" father. He had his flaws like any other man but refused to accept his shortcomings and always placed the blame on the white man. "The white man made me poor." "The white man made my mom smoke crack." "The white man this, and the white man that." He never just kept shit 100. After leaving his home, he pushed his '98 Honda Civic down Cascade Road and got on the highway headed to Grady Memorial Hospital. He found a parking meter that was available and parked. He turned down his radio and said, "Now listen you two, don't get in here and embarrass yo' daddy…please girls." Dre knew his two queens were fierce together and always found a way to get into some type of bullshit.

"Okay Dadeee…" they both said in unison, sounding like little angels.

The day was hot, humid and it didn't help that the air conditioner in his car didn't work. After helping his girls out the car, he held their hands and walked across the busy Atlanta street. The air smelled of trash, gas and stale cigarettes. A blue '72 Chevy Impala drove past sitting on some 32" Forgi's, bumping the new single from Strictlybiz "Yeah I Got Haters." The two girls bobbed their head to the song they'd heard so much on the radio. "This summer I got to get my money up," Dre said to himself.

At 1:25 p.m. they were finally called in to see the doctor who looked like a fat version of Robert Dinero. As McKenzie and Shariya looked curiously around the doctor's office, the doctor chimed in with, "Hey, would you two lovely ladies like some candy?"

They both giggled and said, "Yes sir," at the same time.

While the girls ate their candy the doctor pulled Dre to the side. The girls were too busy eating their candy to pay attention. "Look Andre, I'm going to do this DNA test but I really need you to do the stuff you promised me."

The doctor was one of Dre's old dope friends who loved to snort cocaine. Dre used him for any and everything but after Dre's mother told him the two twin girls didn't resemble him at all, he started noticing the same thing. He knew Veronica wasn't a hood rat, but shit, she also wasn't an angel.

After getting their blood drawn and crying and promising not to tell mommy, they all left the hospital; but not before Dre paid his debt. "All I got is a hundred sack, 'bout 2.5 grams. When you give me the results I got a little more for you."

The greedy doctor didn't care, he just wanted the dope. "Okay, okay give me two days. Now hurry and go."

Dre knew the results could be the candle on the wedding cake, or the dynamite on their relationship. Either way, he wasn't tripping.

* * * * * * * * *

"Me against the world baby, me against the world." Dre stood in front of the gated Esquire Village projects singing one of his favorite Tupac songs. Since moving to the west side of Atlanta shit had been real hectic. This area was known as part of the infamous Bankhead even though it was on Bolton Road. It was a street with three of its own projects and was considered to be under the Bankhead umbrella.

"Shawty, you got a light?" Dre asked the older-looking woman who stood smoking a Newport and placing a CD into her portable Sony disc man headset.

"Damn, lame-ass bitch nigga, that's all you gone ask a bitch for? No name, how I'm doing, just a handout?"

Dre was originally from SWATS, Zone 4, Campbellton Road. He only moved over to the west side of town to help out his grandmother who was getting old. He looked at the peanut butter complexioned woman and laughed, showing two open-faced gold trim around two of his left teeth. "Damn, Ms. Lady. It ain't even like that. You getting at me like I'm some type of fuck-nigga waiting on MARTA."

The woman rolled her eyes, smiling as she looked inside her Dooney and Burke purse. "Nigga, I know you ain't waiting for no damn bus. You been out here three hours, several done passed, plus I see you out here every morning trapping. But don't you think it's time to start hustling off your pager?"

Dre moved a few slabs of crack here and there. He wasn't a baller but he damn sure wasn't broke. He was only trying to stay fresh and help his grandmother with the bills. It didn't help that his raggedy-ass Chevy needed a new part every damn week. Dre was more into playing with a woman's mind, fucking the shit out of her and then getting her for her welfare check, food stamps, tax refund and shit, even her kid's piggy bank money if he could. "Nawl lil buddy, it ain't even like that. I'm just doing me, trying to stay alive in the 95, ya feel me?" After getting her apartment number and promising to come over and smoke a blunt once she got off work, he was all in. He knew who she was and now she needed to know who he was.

Later that night all Dre could hear was, "Oh my fucking Lord, man daddy, give me that dick!; ooh shit, that's my spot!; yes, yes, yes, yes you hitting that thang and you feel so good without the rubber!; yes daddy I'm 'bout to ooohhhh, shit!!" she screamed. Drew was pounding his new juice-box until it was dripping wet. After smoking three blunts of some bamma weed and drinking some cheap-ass Seagrams gin, the woman named Keyosha was all over Dre.

He had knocked on her apartment door and was greeted by a tribe of children who opened the door. "Damn," was all he could say. After a quick count he counted five kids and it didn't help that he heard another baby crying in a back room.

Keyosha came out the bedroom wearing some tight daisy dukes, her bra, house shoes and smoking a Newport. "Y'all lil fuckers get the fuck out my living room, dammit! Why y'all daddies can never keep y'all?"

The three girls and two boys scattered around the room, kicking shit over. Then they hit Dre with the infamous question: "Whatcho name is?" "Whatchu doing?" and "Are you my daddy?" Dre knew he had to fuck and just leave.

The relationship with him and Keyosha had been going on and off for years. She eventually had two more kids which brought her total to eight. For a minute Dre thought he was trapped but when the kids came out looking hella bright-skinned and Mexican looking he was able to breathe more easily. But that still didn't stop him from fucking her without a rubber. However, after meeting Veronica he had to slow down with Keyosha because not only had she "burnt" him five times—three times with Gonorrhea and twice with Chlamydia—but she was a real dingy-ass broad.

* * * * * * * * *

"Ease up on the gas, son. I don't think 5-0 even tripping yo'," Darryl said. As Rain took instructions from Darryl who sat in the back seat trying to comfort a shaken-up Veronica he said to himself, "My boy really getting soft for some pussy. I can't believe this chump-ass nigga put us at risk to spend life in prison for some birdbrain-ass skeezer."

"Yo', pull over at the KFC so Taz and Veronica can trade seats. I think shawty cool now." He looked at Veronica whom he had been trying to get under control for the entire ride. "You good now, ma."

As Taz sat in the front seat, she thought, "Huh, nigga ain't asked me if I'm good but got his hands wrapped around this bitch. Let me find out he done slipped her the digits on the low and I'm going to give that bitch a real ATL ass whooping." Then she looked back at Daryl and Veronica and said, "Aww, you okay girl? Fuck them broke-ass niggas. Darryl, I'ma get in the back with her and let you and Rain ride up here. Ain't no need for me to ride with Darryl. Shit, my girl need me." Taz made this last remark with sarcasm.

Darryl just shook his head cause he felt the jealousy. "Matter of fact Rain, drive to the spot; no more stops," Darryl said.

Taz wanted to scream.

CHAPTER 28

The next day seemed gloomy to Dre who had been up all night smoking blunts of loud and snorting lines of powder. "Damn, this bitch think she gonna play me. It's all good. Wait until I get my bands up and I'm outta here. Fuck her and these kids." Dre was talking to himself but was thrown off by the ringing of his Verizon phone he had under a joint contract with Veronica. He walked away from the glass kitchen table into the living room, looking for his phone. It rang again and he located it on top of his PS4 (PlayStation 4) where he last left it. He was hoping it was Veronica but was disappointed to see the doctor's number on the dimly lit screen. "What the fuck this lame-ass want this early?" After pressing the talk button Dre became rude and irritable. "Mane look, I told you I had the rest. Why the fuck you calling me so early, sweating me?"

The doctor let out a deep breath. "I don't know how to say this but I have bad news and very bad news."

Dre was so high off the raw coke he wasn't even tripping. "Well, spit it out goddammit. You on my daytime minutes and I still owe yo' greedy ass." Dre walked back to where he left his lit blunt and hit it twice.

"Well, the bad news is neither McKenzie or Sariyah are yours, and the very bad news is that you have full blown AIDS. The way I see it is that you've had it quite a while based upon the testing I did with your red and white blood cells. After I got the results back I even retested them myself. I'm sorry," he said. "Our lab returns all blood samples with life-threatening diseases back to us quickly so that we can especially notify the AIDS patients not to donate blood or have unprotected sex, which is the reason I got your results back within twenty-four hours."

The doctor was going on and on but Dre wasn't listening. He already knew who gave him AIDS. Dre hung up the phone and started crying. He knew neither one of his girls favored him, not one bit, but he never entertained the slightest thought they were not his. He couldn't believe Veronica would do something so coldhearted. Dre walked into his precious little girl's room and as he looked at them he smiled in a daze. They were still asleep, like angels...so innocent.

He walked into the bathroom and found two razors. He lowered the toilet lid and sat on it with a razor in each hand and said a prayer. He prayed for his grandma who had died. He poured his heart out for his daughters because he felt like their father, regardless of what the results showed. He now hated Veronica and felt like the Karma was on her for leading him on. As far as Keyosha, he had not seen nor heard from her in years. Rumor was she died from pneumonia. Some said she moved to L.A. and he'd even heard she was fucking Busta Rhymes and got Herpes from Usher. But whatever happened to her, he knew without a doubt she was the one who gave him AIDS. She was messy, nasty and just didn't care. He put the razor to his left wrist. "Lord, forgive me," he whispered as he dug the razor into his skin and closed his eyes.

"Dadeee...I gotta pee!"

CHAPTER 29

"So Sheila, you tellin' me that pussy-ass nigga been lying to me the whole time about my work?" Drill yelled into the phone as he headed over to his home girl, Sheila's house.

"Drill, now you and I both know Doug ain't get robbed for shit. His punk-ass been putting that shit up his nose and that's why he ain't got your money. Now he on some scared shit and trying to move me and Leslie down to Florida with his funky-ass momma who he knows I can't stand."

Sheila was sitting on her porch smoking a black and mild, deceiving and betraying her husband after she found out he was fucking one of her best friends. However, Doug was a good man, a great father and an overall loyal nigga. He never snorted anything up his nose. Hell, he barely smoked weed. The truth of the matter was that Sheila had her brothers, Mar and T Clay from Muncie, Indiana, rob Doug for the $6,000 he owed Drill. They caught Doug slipping as he came out of Sheila's best friend Gena's house for a quick booty call. Doug didn't have to tell Sheila what she already knew. When he got robbed Doug made it seem as if he got robbed at his partner's house. Sheila also knew that while in traffic, Doug had met a new connect named Rain who had promised Doug a nice deal if he was willing to take the bricks on consignment.

"Yeah Drill, and I know he been shopping with some New York nigga named Rain who supposed to be holding major weight. Huh, talk about loyalty."

Drill was furious as he drove the Impala closer to Sheila's crib. "I'll be there in two minutes. Make sure you keep that nigga occupied." As they both hung up their phones, Sheila felt a heavy object graze the side of her head.

"Bitch, you on some foul shit!" Doug yelled as he swung the chrome .44 in Sheila's direction again. Doug had been at the screen door for the last three minutes, listening to Sheila's plot on his life.

As Sheila got her thoughts together she quickly made a dash off the porch which was littered with cigarette butts, old beer cans, Leslie's toys and chipped paint that had fallen off the panels of the house. Not the one to be played, Doug gave chase after Sheila and caught up with her in the middle of the yard. "Awgh fuck!" and he slapped the loaded revolver across her face, instantly breaking her nose and jaw into what sounded like several little pieces. Doug grabbed the back of Sheila's shirt collar and dragged her up the rusted steps, back onto the porch and into the house.

"Leave my mommy alone!" yelled Lil Leslie as she rained punches on her stepfather. Since her birth Doug played daddy but both Drill and Sheila knew this was Lucky's daughter.

The front door was open when Drill pulled up in Sheila's front yard and he was immediately on alert. He grabbed the AR-15 off his backseat and exited the vehicle quickly. He silently crept closer to the front door, not wanting to be caught by surprise but wanting to be the element of surprise.

"Bitch, why you lie to that nigga? You got that nigga thinking I'm some type of sucka-ass nigga playing wit his money. Answer me, bitch!" Doug screamed as he continued to beat on Sheila with the butt of his revolver.

"Fu-fuc-fuck you, nigga! You don't...you don't think I know you fucking Gena? Yeah, punk, my brothers caught yo' sneaky ass coming out her house and stripped yo' soft ass," Sheila said, laughing but crying at the same time with a mouth full of blood. Drill just stood behind the living room wall, listening. "Yeah fag-ass nigga, wait until Drill get here. You got some explaining to do. He know I ain't gonna lie to him so who you think he gone believe? Plus, he already know about that wack-ass New York connect you been talking to."

Doug was sweating heavily as Leslie screamed again, "Leave my mommy alone!" But Doug pulled the big hammer back and laughed, "Fuck you bitch!" BLATT! BLATT... Five shots from Drill's AR-15 tore the upper half of Doug's body to pieces but not before his fingers jerked out of fear and a big BOOM! echoed through the house as the bullet from Doug's large revolver tore a Super Bowl patch of turf out of Sheila's forehead. As the blood and gray-matter splattered all over the room, this sent Lil Leslie running into her bedroom where her television was playing "Barney" very loudly. Little Leslie ran and hid her small body underneath her bed.

Drill, not paying attention to the little girl, was more focused on the location of Sheila's stash spot and any extra money Doug may have had on him. As Drill tore through the kitchen cabinets and drawers, he found what he was looking for in the freezer, wrapped and stuffed into a Popsicle box. It appeared to be a nice stack of hundreds and a few zips of crack. Jackpot! Drill knew he had to hurry. He ran towards the back hall and entered Sheila's master bedroom. The room reeked of dick, ass and balls. The room was also cluttered with old dirty thongs that looked like they hadn't been washed in weeks, bras, dirty gym shoes and half-packed suitcases. "Punk-ass bitch!" he said out loud as he quickly scanned the room, making sure he didn't miss anything of value. "Bingo," he said as he eyed the shiny bling that sat on the dresser. Lifting up the necklace he could see that it was customized with the name "Doug" from the cartoon on "Nickelodeon." Drill ran out of the room and ran toward the front door knowing the po-po was on the way.

But as Drill started to exit the front door he thought he heard a small voice over the loud Barney television show. "Fuck!" he thought as he remembered Sheila's daughter, Leslie. He quietly walked towards the hallway. He had no intentions of hurting the child, he just wanted to make sure he was in the clear. When he looked into the child's bedroom he noticed the Barney DVD was still playing, "Hello kids, say Hi to Barney." He glanced around the room and didn't see anyone. Before he turned around he felt a breeze like a small animal had passed behind him. Out of the corner of his eyes he could see Leslie's pigtails flying around the corner. "Dammit!" he yelled as he gave chase after the young child. He made it down the hallway and past the dead bodies and watched as the child ran out the front door. "Nooo! Leslie no!" But it was too late.

He had to get out of there. He ran from the house and heard sirens then he saw the lights of a single squad car coming up the street. Drill quickly ran to the driver's side of his '96 Impala, laid the AR-15 on his lap and started the engine. However, before he got a chance to get out the driveway, the cop jumped out of the squad car with his service revolver drawn.

"Freeze! Step out of the car!" the young white officer ordered. He wondered where his backup was. As he reached for his radio to call for more assistance, he was greeted with a burst of hot shells. BLAHHH! BLAHHH! Drill stood outside the door of his Impala, letting the 100-round drum on his AR-15 talk for him. Drill kept two or three weapons on him at all times. He refused to be robbed or arrested.

The young rookie cop immediately jumped into his squad car and tried to put it in reverse. Little Leslie, who had been hiding in the bushes, ran to the passenger side of the cop's car and tried to open the door. The rookie officer didn't see her as he wildly swung the car around, knocking the little girl down. Her leg broke on impact and she appeared unconscious. Drill chased the car as the officer drove the car in reverse wildly. He lifted the AR-15 and let off another 20 rounds at the front windshield. Then he ran back to his Chevy, seeing as neighbors were looking out their windows, some screaming. He walked over to Leslie and looked at her lifeless body. He felt her wrist for a pulse, but shit he wasn't a doctor and didn't know if she was dead or alive. He jumped back into his Impala and floored it down the street.

As his radio blasted Philthy Phil's "1st Day Out," Drill stopped at the squad car, extended his arm out the driver side window and pumped five more shots out of his 9mm into the injured cop's upper body. He accelerated on the gas and was met at the street sign by three more squad cars. "Fuck it! I'm going out blazing!" Drill said and grabbed a pack of Newports off his dashboard, shook one out and lit it. *"Nigga, I came from nuttin'; no food in my stomach; now it's 454's and 600's they all runnin'."* "1st Day Out" screamed out his 6x9 speakers. Drill reached under his seat and grabbed two more 100-round drums. He ejected the first drum out of the AR-15 and reloaded as he watched several more cop cars gather and surround his vehicle. He knew he needed a miracle to make it out alive so he said a quick prayer, knowing God probably wouldn't answer him anyway. He finished and said, "Amen."

Twelve to fifteen officers stood with their guns drawn. "Put down the weapon. This is your last warning!" the police Captain yelled through a bullhorn.

"Fuck y'all pussy-ass crackers!" Drill let the clip go as he hung out the window of his Impala. He swung the blower like a ball bat. The excessive fire power had most, if not all, the officers running for cover. "Yeah, pussies, run!" Drill yelled. BLATTT! BLATTT! BLATTT! BLATTT! He put the Impala in reverse and decided to take another route. He floored the engine and although he spun out of control for a moment, he had a firm grip on the steering wheel and trigger of his AR-15. He drove 130 mph down the quiet street of his victim's neighborhood. He had glanced in the direction where he last saw Leslie's body but it was now gone. As the squad cars raced behind him he called the only person he knew. He placed the AR-15 on the passenger seat while calling Lucky. He had a good chance of getting away if he had a plan. When he dialed Lucky's number, they both spoke at the same time, "Mane, you ain't gone believe this!"

* * * * * * * * *

"Put your hands up where I can see them!" After crashing his Impala while trying to make a sharp turn, the game had finally ended for Drill. Lucky was still on the phone and heard the loud sound of a BOOM! but didn't know and couldn't tell exactly what it was. Drill, who wasn't wearing a seatbelt, was lucky his airbag released and saved him.

"Agggh…Agggh…" Drill moved around like a drunken man still in shock from the impact of the crash.

"I said put your fuckin' hands up, now!" the black officer screamed as he pointed a black .40 cal. so close to Drill he could read the serial number on it. Drill, who was halfway unconscious, didn't understand anything as he drifted away, closing his eyes…

* * * * * * * * *

"Ronneal, why do you always talk crazy to me like that?" Melina had been dating Ronneal "Drill" Dawkins since he moved to Indiana from Texas.

"Bitch, cause you my bitch and that's just how it is. Now roll up a blunt and fix me another drink." Young Ronneal had been staying with his father and grandfather on 21ˢᵗ and Bellefountaine for the past two years since his mama shipped his bad ass off to Indiana. His father, who really wanted nothing to do with him, sent him to his auntie in Muncie, Indiana where Ronneal was born. But living in the Munsyanna Homes projects in Crosstown wasn't gone cut it. Ronneal fought all the kids in the projects. Some were his cousins because they said, "Nigga, you ain't from here no mo'." So after two weeks he moved back with his dad.

"Look son, um, I mean Neal, oh what the hell. Look boy, you on your own. I'm giving you a free roof over ya head but you're damn near a man, so it's all on you to feed yourself." With that being said, Ronneal started hustling, busting guns and getting money.

One day after washing his '79 Delta 88 on triple-gold Daytons, he met Melina at the Shell gas station. It was a hot, humid day and the sun was blazing at a high 98 degrees. Ronneal had just finished putting black magic on his Vogue tires. "Mr. Ice Cream man…Master P the Ice Cream man" was pounding from his two 15's in the trunk. As Melina walked out of the Shell station with a grape Faygo soda in one hand and a bag of hot Cheetos in the other, young Ronneal knew he had to have her.

"Aye, what's up wit it?" he yelled from his car. Melina just rolled her eyes and kept walking. "Ugh, back up off me, ugh back up off me. T-R-U we true, ugh," his Alpine blasted as he pulled up next to Melina.

"Boy, turn that shit down. Damn, a bitch can't even think straight!" Melina yelled over the loud stereo system.

Roneal turned his music down and Melina walked over to his old-school. "Just get in. You smoke? I got that doedie right now. Get in baby girl."

Melina raced her lil fast-ass over to the passenger side. That night they fucked and got high, but Ronneal was a player and Melina was scandalous.

"Like I said, bitch, fix me another drink and roll up a blunt while I count this money."

After two years with Ronneal, Melina had enough. He wasn't physically abusive, just talked a lot of shit. But Melina came from a scandalous household. "Girl, when that nigga keep talking that shit, slip his ass a mickey," her older cousin Tywanie told her. She explained all you had to do was drop 6 to 7 drops of Visine into his drink and it would knock him out. So after making his drink and stirring it with her finger, she thought about just pouring the spiked drink out and leaving him. "What if it don't work? What if he finds out?" Those were the questions she asked herself.

"Damn, you took a long time. What did you do, poison me or something?" Ronneal said as he grabbed the drink out of her hand. Melina almost pissed on herself with his last comment. He saw her expression and said, "Bitch, I'm talking shit. I know yo' dumb-ass wouldn't know poison from candy, ha-ha." Ronneal threw the drink back into his mouth and swallowed all the contents. At first he felt nothing at all, but within 15 minutes he was sound asleep. When he woke up he was at Wishard Hospital.

"Young man, how do you feel? You probably don't know but you've been hospitalized for 3½ weeks in an induced coma. Your grandfather is in the lobby now. He's been by your bedside the whole time."

Ronneal was dazed as he slowly moved around in the bed. "Wh…what about my da…dad? Where's my pops?"

The young doctor took a deep breath and thought wisely before choosing his words. The room Drill had been assigned was small and had that disinfectant smell to it. "Your dad, well I'll just be honest, your dad didn't even want us to revive you when you went into cardiac arrest. He requested we not send the hospital bill to him. I'm sorry."

That's when Ronneal's grandfather walked in. At 82-years old Mr. Jambro Dawkins still looked fit except for the wrinkles in his face and a head full of gray hair. The man still maintained a certain swagger. "Boy, wake yo' ass up," Mr. Dawkins said, and playfully punched Drill in the arm. Since moving to Indiana, his grandpa Jambro had showed him nothing but love; real unconditional.

"Mr. Dawkins, as I explained to you earlier, we found that your grandson had ingested a very strong dosage of a substance only found in the eye product, Visine. So at this point we feel he was either purposely poisoned or he intentionally swallowed the substance. Drill tried to sit up but he couldn't. His hands were cuffed to the bed railing.

That's when two detectives walked into the room and said, "Ronneal Dawkins, you are under arrest for the murder of Melina Gomez." They read him his Miranda rights and went on to explain that Melina was found dead next to his unconscious body. A .38 Special was lying next to her body but it had both his and Melina's fingerprints on it.

"Oh Lawd, I'm...I'm...I....!" his grandpa called out, his face contorted in pain as he clutched his chest while falling to the floor, knocking over IV monitors and other medical equipment.

"Papa, papa!" Ronneal yelled as the young doctor bent down to assist Mr. Dawkins.

"He's having a heart attack! Officer, pick up the phone on that table and tell the front desk operator to contact the head doctor on call, NOW!" the young doctor ordered urgently. He jabbed a code into his pager at his waist. The old Asian detective finished the call to the front desk just as several doctors and technicians rushed into the room to help escort Mr. Dawkins via stretcher out of the room. A tech restored order to the knocked over equipment. Then the last doctor finally left the room and closed the door, leaving a cuffed Ronneal crying and screaming with the two detectives.

"Now you listen and you listen good; we want all the details of how this happened," the young Asian detective whispered to Ronneal with the stale smell of Newports on his breath.

"I…I didn't do nothing." The doctor had given Ronneal a shot to calm him before he left the room and it was beginning to take effect. His speech was slurred and then interrupted by heavy breathing as he began to fall asleep.

The young detective reached around the IV's and placed his pale hands around Ronneal's neck, choking his Adam's apple aggressively. Ronneal shook uncontrollably in his bed, making gagging noises like *"Agggh…agggh…uggghh…"*

The older detective, who favored Brett Favre in his earlier days, stood guard at the door and watched out for any nurse or doctor who got curious and wanted to come into the room where a man had a heart attack while visiting. He said, *"That's enough Nygen. This fucker's got enough on his plate."*

After several months of trial, Ronneal was found guilty by reason of insanity and sent to a mental hospital in Richmond, Indiana to complete his four-year sentence for manslaughter. However, the truth was that his grandpa, Jambro, was the actual killer. After going into the kitchen to get his whiskey, he saw the Visine container sitting next to the Grey Goose. He'd observed Melina give the drink to his grandson, so he did what he had to do. But the secret died with him in the hospital. No one ever knew the truth.

CHAPTER 30

As the humid Houston air blew through the open balcony door of the plush hotel in downtown Houston, Kilo looked around and smiled, admiring the elegance of the penthouse suite he was occupying for the All-Star weekend. He stood up and stretched out his 5'2" frame and slightly brushed the wrinkles out of his crème Armani suit. "Life is good, life is good," he repeated as he walked out on the balcony. As the midnight wind blew, Kilo's hair danced with the air. Being born black and Arabian had its advantages. He kept his hair shoulder-length and groomed into a wet-looking, curly style. Some, if not most people, have mistaken him for Mexican, Cuban or some other descent of that type.

He slowly inhaled his expensive cigar and spoke aloud, "All this money Darryl's bringing in, I may have to make him part of the team." Kilo wasn't some urban book kingpin with thousands and thousands of bricks, hit men, yachts and jets. He was a boss who knew how to make the proper investments. Aside from his clothing store in New York, soul food restaurant in Phoenix and auto parts store in Georgia, Kilo pushed bamma weed, purple, cush, ecstasy pills and cocaine in bulks. He was the connect Darryl thought he was being hooked up with. After serving nearly a dime in the feds, he never revealed his position to buyers. He had his clientele thinking he was the middle man and allowed his son to take all the credit and exposure as being the man in charge. RuTristen, who was 23-years old, was the spittin' image of his father but just a tad bit cockier.

* * * * * * * * *

Ru cut back on the "flashy" image his father warned him about after being laced day after day, year after year. "Son, the guys with the ice, Bentleys and chinchillas are the ones the feds watch. The working man in the Honda who stays off the radar is the one who gets rich and enjoys the fruits of his labor. Now take the Lamborghini back!"

Young Tristen was furious that year but as he watched all his competition get indictments he later thanked his father. "Yeah, yeah old man, you were right."

Kilo never got a chance to be a real father to young Tristen while doing eight years in the feds. It seemed like yesterday when the feds stormed into his church house while young RuTristen was being baptized. The preacher was saying, "And I hereby baptize this child in the name of…" BOOM!

"Get the fuck down! FBI!" A federal team of agents moved in quickly with pistols and high-powered assault rifles drawn. "Down NOW!!" As several agents moved in to apprehend RuTristen "Kilo" Movan, Sr., a barrage of shots echoed in the church house. BLAAHH! BLAAHH! BLAAHH! BOOM! BOOM! BOOM! Two agents were caught off guard as three men in white suits unloaded their magazines at the agents. The third agent was a black female who returned fire from two .40 calibers. BOOM! BOOM! BOOM! BOOM! She continued to clutch until the hot shells reached their targets. The first man hit was Kilo's brother as two bullets turned his white linen to Kool-Aid red and a 3rd bullet opened his forehead, splattering his brains onto the old lady next to him which was his mother.

"Aggh…Aggh…Aggh!" the 79-year old woman screamed as her oldest son shook his life away into the depths of hell. Kilo, who had just watched his only sibling get murdered, ran for his son. BOOM! BOOM! BOOM! The female agent fired away. BLAAHH! BLAAHH! BLAAHHHHHH! The AR-15 the preacher held sounded off as he took out two more agents. The preacher, who was actually Kilo's father and connect, always kept heavy artillery in the house of God. His motto was, "I'd rather be safe than sorry." Actually, this church was the headquarters of his

drug operation. With a burial ground on the church's four acres of land, this was the perfect place to manufacture, distribute and stash large amounts of cocaine. With over 50 tombstones and caskets buried, there were more than dead bodies six feet deep out there. More like guns, cocaine, money, passports and fake I.D.'s. For every dead person buried there was a new identity to be used.

"You disrespect the house of God. Is that what you want? War?" BLAAHHH! BLAAHH! BLAAHHHH! The female agent ran towards Kilo and her vest ate every bit of 15 shells, knocking the wind out of her.

Kilo's mother was screaming as she held her oldest son in her arms as she crooned, "Poor baby, poor baby. You will fly with the angels now."

Kilo was in the midst of grabbing his son out of the small baptismal pool of water when he felt a hand on his shoulder. "Son, let's hurry and go! There are more pigs coming!" BOOM! BOOM! BOOM! The shots from the front entrance caught Kilo's father and the three shots ripped through the tissue of his stomach. He dropped his gun and looked down at his stomach where his intestines were falling out. Not believing his eyes he looked up at his shooter, or shooters, and smiled at a fourth bullet blasted through his right eye socket. As the back of his head exploded and painted the air red, Kilo's mother, Martha, had a sudden heart attack. Kilo looked at his mother, father and brother while clutching his son and it all made him come back to his senses. "Mama, no!" he whispered as he ran toward his mother's body as it lay twisted on the church house floor.

"Freeze! Don't fucking move," he heard the female agent yell between deep breaths. A swarm of agents moved in to cut off Kilo as he held his son and his mother with both arms.

"Call the ambulance! My mama's dying!" Kilo shouted between sobs. "Call the damn ambulance!" he roared with the bass of a lion.

"Call, call the ambulance? Ha-ha, are you fucking serious?" the female agent said as she took deep breaths. Even though the bullets hadn't penetrated her vest, they had knocked a substantial amount of air out of her lungs.

As young Tristen was pried from Kilo's arms, he cried, screamed and yelled at the top of his young lungs. While being cuffed by two agents and surrounded by the Phoenix Police Department, Kilo looked down at his mother who was still breathing and cried out, "Please, please save my mama."

The white police officers reached for their radios to call an ambulance. "Are you interfering with federal matters, huh? Because all I see is dead federal...all I see is dead federal agents. There's no need for an ambulance. Let this bitch die. She birthed Satan," the female agent said to the local officers. She was right. This was federal jurisdiction and no one liked cop killers.

"Shit, it's your call, lady," one said as they escorted Kilo outside to an unmarked fed car; Kilo vowed to seek revenge for his mother.

As the female agent bent down inside the church, she smelled death in the air. Blood was splattered everywhere. Brain matter was on the floors and here sat a woman who was still alive. "Do you want me to call an ambulance?" she whispered to the old lady. The woman shook her head, no. "Bitch, do you want an ambulance?" the agent asked again. And again the old lady shook her head, no. But Kilo's mom was a soldier. She didn't have a heart attack but faked one, knowing her son wouldn't retaliate because he would be too worried about her. She also knew the church ran a 24-hour surveillance camera that was recording at all times. Kilo's father had it set up to watch for anything suspicious. She knew her son would never be charged with hurting anyone and that's why she'd faked the heart attack.

"Oh, you'se a tuff lady; a tuff lil bitch, huh?" the agent whispered as she looked around. She heard the sirens of the ambulances and fire trucks and expected them to come a long time ago. As she scanned the room again, agents were picking up weapons and checking the pulses of the bodies lying around in the aftermath of catastrophic mayhem left in that church. "Don't trip bitch.

Y'all shot at the wrong bitch today," the agent continued to whisper while applying pressure to the windpipe of the old lady. "That's right…kick bitch…yeah…kick…and when you get to hell, tell that husband of yours I send mines."

As Kilo's mom kicked and floated into "the end of the road," it was almost as if Kilo felt it and shed a tear in the back of the vehicle. As he looked out the window, he watched the female agent as she stepped out of the church and spit in the flowerbed his mother had planted. They both made eye contact at the same time. "You may want to call an ambulance. I believe there's someone with a pulse in there," she called out sarcastically to the officers as two ambulances pulled up. She swayed her body back and forth as she walked towards the unmarked vehicle. She stared at Kilo through the window then with aggressive force she opened the back door. "Oh, look at ya. Yeah, mama's gone now; but don't worry, we'll put your bastard son in a real nice foster home until he's 18 and I'll make sure you get life," the agent vowed.

But after two and a half years and $200,000 in lawyer fees, Kilo was acquitted on every murder charge. The videotape which would have proven his innocence was mysteriously lost. But his father was a smart man and Kilo revealed the second monitor's hiding place to his attorney for an additional $50,000 bonus. After the video surfaced the community was in shock. Old folks who knew Pastor Danny knew he was a crook, but this "took the cake."

The female agent was honored with medals and promotions based on her heroic efforts because the video showed her only speaking to Kilo's mother and placing her hand on her neck which was normal protocol when checking for a pulse. She came off looking like a saint. They charged Kilo with unlawful possession of a firearm with a scratched off serial number that was found in his car in the church's parking lot, along with 2,016 grams of powdered cocaine. He was sentenced to 120 months in the fed pen. His son, RuTristen Jr., was returned to Kilo's wife who was the biological mother. While in County locked up and awaiting trial, he was refused the right to attend his *families' funerals. But he knew once he was released he was a wealthy man. Not only did his father have over 10 kilograms in those buried caskets, his mother's and father's life insurance policies combined totaled $3 million dollars. As well as cocaine, his father left behind several business blueprints, $2.2 million dollars in cash, a slew of vehicles (old and new), an arsenal of weapons and a son with a broken heart.*

* * * * * * * * *

As Kilo stood on the hotel balcony inhaling his cigar, his cellphone exploded with his 2Pac ringtone "Ain't Nuttin' but a Gangsta Party." He raced back into the suite. He was waiting on Darryl's call to make sure the transaction went smoothly. "My friend, hello," Kilo greeted him. He could hear yelling and more in the background.

"I need a place to cool off, O.G. I'm hot right now," Darryl replied.

"Dammit D, what have you gotten into? My peoples hooked you up, yeah." Kilo used a scrambler on his phone to avoid any wiretaps or taped conversations. He refused to go back to prison.

"Nawl, we good on that. Matter of fact I'm still riding dirty…fuck…aye Rain, we gone have to drop this shit off. Fuck, I'm trippin'," Darryl yelled into the phone. Taz whispered something into Darryl's ear about leaving whatever he had in her room. "Quick thinking, ma… damn, a nigga love you for that." Darryl smiled while Rain mugged him in the rearview mirror. "Son, turning into a fruitcake," he said to himself. "Yo, Kilo…I mean K…give me a few minutes." But the phone went dead and Darryl immediately knew why. Kilo had told him many times that he was an old head and out of the game but to never mention his name outside of prison walls and never by phone or face-to-face! When Darryl called back it went straight to voicemail. "Fuck it!

We're still going to O.G.'s room once we drop this shit off," he said. Darryl eyeballed Taz who at the moment was acting weird.

"Whatever the fuck y'all niggas got, let's just go to my room," Taz suggested. "Fuck O.G., Kilo, Kemo or whatever his name is. Fuck!" Then she rolled down the window to get some fresh air.

Meanwhile, back in his suite, Kilo was fuming! "Muthafucka...I tell him...never say my name and what does he do? He says my name!!" Kilo threw his phone into the wall, watching as it exploded into a thousand pieces. "I need a fuckin' drink. Yes, that's it..." he said as he checked his watch. He headed for the door but not before tucking his twin Desert Eagles into his Armani slacks. Maybe I'm being too paranoid, he wondered as he walked out the door and headed for the penthouse elevator.

* * * * * * * * *

"Yo, son, fuck what she talking 'bout. We headed to old head's room down the street. Stick to the script till the heat die down, remember?" Rain yelled as he gave orders while Darryl, Taz and Veronica all exited the Hotel Derek.

"I'm just saying we can get another room somewhere else and chill," Taz chimed in.

Veronica was still woozy and hadn't said much. Rain thought she was still a little shell-shocked.

"You right, captain. We got too much to lose," Darryl said as he finally gave in. Veronica rolled her eyes again. Rain thought he really ran the world and that was the biggest turn-off for her.

* * * * * * * * *

As Kilo downed his 3rd shot of Cognac, he checked his Breitling watch again. He knew Darryl would show up and that was the bad part. He knew Darryl was not only hardheaded but inconsiderate. Kilo used the lounge and bar of the hotel as his hideaway so he could watch the entrance. Maybe he would slap the shit out of Darryl or maybe cut him off. He didn't know. He looked up and there was Darryl coming through the door with three other people.

* * * * * * * * *

"Look, my boy K ain't too fond of new people so y'all chill at the bar while me and Rain go talk to him. We can get a few rooms here if they're not filled up. My boy got the hookup."

"Well, I ain't got that much cash on me so, um, I guess you or Rain may need to come off a few bills," Veronica stated.

"Rain, go buy them a few drinks and something to eat. You know the room number. Plus, it would be best if I talk to my boy. He kind of pissed at me."

"No doubt, son. I got you." Rain gave Darryl a fist pound and walked the two fine women to the bar.

As Kilo tipped the bartender he bobbed his head to the vibrant sounds of Whitney Houston's "I Will Always Love You" that played smoothly over the lounge area's speakers. "Such a tragic loss; rest in peace, girl," Kilo mumbled as he stood up and had to catch his balance. It seemed when he turned around he saw the Devil in 3D. Kilo reached under his crème Armani shirt and yanked out the two twin Desert Eagles. BOOM! BOOM! BOOM! BOOM! BOOM! BOOM! The loud shots woke the hotel up! The lounge area was in complete pandemonium. But Kilo kept clutching. BOOM! BOOM!

As Darryl waited for the elevator, he was smacked out of his thoughts by the sounds of what he knew was gunfire. "What the fuck?" All he could think about was that Rain might have put Taz's life in danger. But when he ran to the lounge area he couldn't believe what he saw.

* * * * * * * * *

"Fuck! You wilding out, son?" Rain yelled as he responded back to the shots with a full clip of his own. BANG! POP! POP! BANG! POP! POP! POP! POP! Rain was confused. He didn't know if dude was drunk or just gung ho. "Veronica and Taz, stay the fuck down!" Rain let off six more shots before realizing he had an empty clip in his .40 cal. "Fuck!" he yelled. BOOM! BOOM! The two shots caught Rain off guard and lifted him into the air and onto a couch in the lounge area. The bright green couch was now covered with Rain's blood and now resembled a big watermelon.

"Rain, nooo…!" Darryl yelled as he ran toward his best friend. As Kilo stepped out the bar area he ran toward his intended targets: Veronica and Taz. As he raised both pistols to fire, the entrance of the lounge and bar exploded with the Houston Police Department drug task force, DEA and FBI agents.

"Put down the muthafuckin' gun right now!" an agent screamed at Kilo.

Darryl was watching everything unfold like a movie, holding on to Rain's chest as blood poured out quickly. "I'm…I'm good son. Get the work. That's…that's too many meal tic…tick…tickets…" Rain gurgled as blood started flowing from his mouth. "Go…" he mumbled to Darryl who reluctantly got up and slowly blended into the crowd of onlookers and hotel staff. He made his way to the door that read "emergency exit."

"Bitch, you thought you'd never see the Devil again, huh? You thought it was over!" BOOM!! Kilo got off one shot before being riddled with shells from every type of weapon you could imagine: pumps, Rugers, high-powered rifles, 9mms, etc.

As Kilo fell to the ground, he looked into the eyes of the woman who had caused him so much pain and misery. "Fuck you, bitch!" were his last words.

* * * * * * * * *

As Veronica lay on the operating table at Houston's main hospital, Kilo lay in the operating room next to hers, barely clinging to his life. Beep, Beep, Beep, Beep, Beep. "She's losing too much blood. Let's hurry up and get that bullet out of her!" the doctor yelled as he gave orders to remove the bullet lodged in Veronica's neck. As Taz waited outside of Veronica's room she told herself that tonight had been one hell of a night. She definitely didn't expect the turn of events to transpire into this. As the agents from the FBI asked her if she needed anything, she just rolled her eyes and thought about Darryl. "Nigga should have listened to me."

* * * * * * * * *

"Ms. Vasquez, the boss wants to see you," the young FBI agent, Darbuck Brown, said sarcastically. "Ohhh…you in trouble," her senior partners in the agency said playfully. Actually, they all knew she was getting promoted and was going to be the head of the Georgia Branch of the FBI which also worked with the GBI (Georgia Bureau of Investigations) after taking down RuTristen "Kilo" Movan, Sr. years ago. This was long overdue.

As Ms. Vasquez walked into her boss' office it smelled like pork rinds with a mixture of Bengay and cheap cologne. "Yessss?" she replied with a smile as she walked over to his desk, playfully running her finger across the rosewood desk, blinking her eyelashes like a little girl.

"You can stop all the Hollywood shit. You know you got the promotion and will be relocating to your hometown in Georgia. As you know, Mr. Movan will be released soon. We are planning on keeping a close eye on him. We never recovered any money, drugs, or weapons from his father's properties. So that leaves me to believe they have some type of stash house. But word is from one of our CI's (confidential informant) housed in the same federal institution he's in is that he's recruiting a team of young hustlers. Now that's where you come in," the fat, out of shape, pale white man said, pointing his stubby finger at Ms. Vasquez.

"Moi...me..." she said.

"Yes, you. You will go into deep cover, keeping your eyes and ears open; even your legs if you have to. I want to keep tabs on anybody in his housing unit that's getting out and I want them watched closely. This is going to be big, you watch and see."

Ms. Vasquez rolled her eyes. The FBI had performed a profile on her so she was sure they knew she'd been through counseling for being raped. But her scores were so high in training they couldn't deny her the position. She hated dope and everything that came with it. She had lost her mother and father to cocaine. She felt any man who dealt drugs was a total scumbag and if she could she would take them all down. "Alright boss, what you need from me? I'm all in." She sat down in the plush brown leather chair.

"Okay Taz, it's like this..." he began.

* * * * * * * * *

Taz snapped out of her daydream of how it started with her. She looked down the hallway to see a younger version of Kilo arguing with officers. "This is my fuckin' dad! Let me see my dad!" young Tristen yelled. It took two officers to calm him down but not before having to place him in cuffs.

Taz had to admit the young man had taste and was handsome. Kilo had been under 24-hour around the clock surveillance for the past year or so. The case they were building on him was a very difficult one because they could never catch him in the act. But Taz knew he had his hand in the cookie jar and after the young man identified himself as his son, she thought to herself, "like father like son." The Houston branch was aware of Taz and had done a great job of not blowing her cover at the scene of the hotel shootout. She just prayed Kilo stayed in critical condition long enough for her to finish her investigation. Not only had Kilo built a drug empire, he had begun to traffic young females from the Middle East and used them not only as female prostitutes, but as drug transporters, setup artists and for many identity theft scams. Okay, it was time to go to work.

Taz walked up to Tristen and said, "Baby boy, calm down. You alright, sexy?" She wrapped her arms around his shoulders after he was uncuffed.

"Sir, you and your lady friend will have to wait to see this man. He is under federal custody," the officer stated.

As Tristen looked up with tears in his eyes, he looked at Taz. She was beautiful but she had a look in her eyes he knew from somewhere; he just couldn't put a finger on it. "Nawl baby, I'm good. I just need some fresh air that's all."

As they walked out of the hospital together, Taz said a quick prayer for Veronica who jumped in front of the bullet that could have ended Taz's life. "You hungry? I'm hungry, love." They did more than eat that late night and into the morning. Taz fucked Tristen's brains out and let him fuck hers out as well. She had a job to do and the pieces were finally falling into place.

CHAPTER 31

"Dinnertime, nigger boy," the Correctional Officer yelled through the bars as he slid Lavern "Rain" Jordan a tray with a red-looking glob covered in what Rain suspected was semen.

"You eat this shit, you pig!" Rain yelled as he slid the tray out of the open slot, causing it to land on the reformatory's porcelain floors and splatter on the dull green walls. Rain, who was now 17, was considered to be "institutionalized." That is, he programmed himself to feel no more pain. Even when he got word his mother died in a house fire while he was locked up, he never shed a tear. He had what you would call a "dangerous mind." He was too unpredictable and unstable.

So Rain plotted as he sat in his boxers on his bed and he hoped his plan worked. He knew Sweeney had been demoted from Sergeant to the lowest rank based on too many investigations for brutality, and he had a temper and would take the bait. Rain had been putting his plan together for two years. He was tired of being beaten, dehumanized, threatened and ridiculed. Several CO's even attempted to rape him but he would just shit on himself after purposely drinking spoiled milk. As Rain fingered the two small shanks under his mattress supplied by Bob Barker, the bars to his cell clicked open.

"Okay, smart-ass, up against the wall."

Rain grabbed and cuffed the shanks while standing up. Many boys behind the walls stashed shanks in their socks, drawers, shirts and even their ass; survival first, questions last. They would push the handle up their ass and leave the sharp end hanging out so they wouldn't damage their insides. No one looked at this as gay or being a fag; it was kill or be killed.

"Okay boy, now bend over. And if you shit today I'm gone just use it as lubricant. I'm gonna teach you a lesson today," Sweeney whispered.

Rain laughed. "Okay Sweeney, just don't be ruff." This response caught Sweeney off guard.

"Oh, so you is a little sweet cake. All this time you been wanting old Sweeney to yourself, boy." Rain bent over and as Sweeney attempted to penetrate him, Rain did a quick twist of his body and swung his fist. All you heard was a loud scream: "Aaaggghhhhhh!!" Sweeney backed up and held his stomach which was covered in blood. "What the fuck?"

Then Rain quickly pulled the second shank out of his boxers and ran toward Sweeney and began to stab him repeatedly in the stomach and face. Sweeney looked up in fear and all he saw was a vicious animal attacking him. And after several officers beat Rain to a pulp, he was taken to a hospital in Manhattan for his life-threatening injuries. He survived, but Sweeney wasn't so lucky. He was pronounced dead at the scene. After an investigation by Internal Affairs and other agencies, Rain was acquitted of murder and ordered to be released immediately after his recovery in the hospital. Sweeney had forgotten about the many cameras which captured his repeated abuse of Rain.

While attending one of the counseling sessions in the hospital's victim unit, he met the one person he trusted for the first time. Seeing this guy move around on crutches looked funny but Rain didn't crack one joke. "What you say your name was again, son?" Rain asked the tall, brown-skinned brother who had bandages wrapped around both knees.

"D...Dub...Darryl Washington, yo'."

* * * * * * * * *

Sosa had received several text messages from Darryl informing him that he was in trouble and needed Sosa to meet him at another location. Sosa was only looking to take a few bricks off Darryl's hands, not to hustle with him. Sosa, like everyone else, had his own hidden agenda.

"Men, follow my cue when we get to the hotel. Remember, there are many innocent bystanders. Like I said, Darryl is no threat. It's his boy, Mr. Rain Jordan, we have to subdue quickly."

As Detective Bernis Yipps aka Sosa gave instructions everyone listened attentively. Bernis had currently been in the drug unit of the Houston Police Department for six years. His street swag and dress code allowed him to rub shoulders with many hustlers and rappers as well as low budget sports players who were moving large amounts of drugs. After witnessing the mayhem at the hotel, he knew his ass was on the line as well as his job. He explained to his superiors that he "never" contacted the FBI. It seemed as if they were doing their own investigation. It was just a coincidence they showed up and it was a tragedy, too, because now the case they had been building against Darryl and Rain was in jeopardy of being in the FBI's hands. Whoever this Kilo guy was, he had fucked up Detective Yipp's 15 minutes of fame.

However, after purchasing small amounts of cocaine from local hustlers and then busting them, a fed ratted out Darryl as the supplier from New York who was trying to expand his empire down south. After being promised freedom, one dealer promised to hook Detective Yipps up with Darryl during All-Star weekend and the rest would be history. Darryl was smarter than he looked. He allowed Detective Yipps to kick it with him, blow a few blunts but he never discussed business as far as cocaine was concerned. It wasn't until the day at the mall Darryl peeped Sosa's rubber band game and his swag and finally concluded: dude was cool. Darryl explained to Sosa that he would hit him with a brick or two just to see how fast he moved it.

Rain was totally against allowing any new niggas into the circle. "Son, you trippin'. This nigga could be on some New Jack City shit for all we know. We don't need his few thousand dollars," Rain stated furiously. Half of his protest was the truth and the other half jealousy. He'd watched Sosa blow money the entire week like it was water plus, Rain didn't want no nigga trying to take his.

"Nigga, I'm the bread-breaker. I put all this shit into play," Darryl pointed out. "Fuck thousands, I'm talking millions. Once this nigga cops from us we gone move into his territory real slow, start feeding his goons, then rock his ass to sleep and take over. That's how we gone play all these country bumpkins, even yo' Dallas boys. So get with the program and play your position." Darryl looked directly into Rain's eyes as he spoke to him.

Rain could have rocked Darryl to sleep years ago. He'd watched as his boy counted millions and stashed brick after brick. Although Rain believed in loyalty, he also believed in rat-ass niggas. "It's good, yo', but let me clarify something." That day at the Cheesecake Factory Rain let his feelings show as he talked to Sosa. "I'm just gone get it off my chest. I think you're a live cornball, clown-ass nigga. You ain't no Sosa. So if you sneeze, breathe or so much as fart wrong and I smell it, I'm your worst nightmare from this day forward. Sweet dreams." Rain mugged Sosa with violent eyes. But Sosa showed not one ounce of fear. He knew the bogeyman and it wasn't Rain.

* * * * * * * * *

"Bernice, Bernice sleeping by the furnace!" all the fourth grade students shouted on the playground at recess.

"Shut up! Leave me alone!" Bernis cried. *After letting his friend, Jamario, spend the night, he was the talk of the school.*

"Man, his house was hella cold. They ain't even got no heat. We had to sleep by an electric furnace and they got roaches. Bernis the furnace! Ha-ha-ha!"

When he came home that day crying, his uncle—who was also his babysitter—told him he was a sissy. "You soft-ass lil bitch! Quit all that crying 'for I give your ass something to cry about." That same day Bernis' uncle whipped him with a hanger and made him sit in scalding hot water he'd boiled on the stove. When Bernis complained about the water being too hot, his uncle shoved him into the tub and kept him there. The dude was a real live crack-head and bad with issues.

Bernis didn't know his father and mother were dead. So he lived with his grandma who always left to play Bingo on Mondays. This day would forever be known as "Monster Monday" because his uncle would make up a reason to get mad just to torture him. He would make him watch scary movies with the lights off; then he would leave and run back into the living room with a hockey mask on and a knife in his hand and chase the young terrified boy around the house. He would gather up roaches in a jar and while Bernis was asleep, he would pour them all over his body and bed and watched as the young boy scratched his poor skin away. Eventually his uncle died in a mysterious house fire on one of those Monday nights. To this day no one expected foul play, but Bernis and his grandma knew the truth. She told him, "I brought my son into this world and I took him out!" Bernis vowed to never fear man again.

CHAPTER 32

Dre was startled and dropped the razor. He yelled out his frustration, "Fuck!" His daughter was at the bathroom door.

"Da…deee! I gotta pee!"

Dre looked down at the small gash on his left wrist. "Damn, I got to get these babies out this house," he thought. Dre flushed the toilet twice and stood up. "Hold on, here I come, baby" he said in a flat, dull tone. All the life, joy and happiness had drained out of him. As he reached to open the medicine cabinet, he looked at himself in the mirror and shook his head.

* * * * * * * * *

Two hours and three blunts later, Dre sat in the living room of Veronica's aunt, Teronda. "So I see her little fast-ass done went and took her ass to the All-Star weekend, huh? I don't know what you see in that hussy," Ronda said as she rolled up another blunt.

After feeding the girls and putting them to bed, Dre and Ronda drank a few shots of Vodka and smoked a few blunts. Dre's mind was in the gutter; he had pain in his heart. Ronda only added to the fuel by speaking recklessly about her niece that she turned her back on after her sister died; how she hated Paco, Veronica's father; how even after the courts gave her the opportunity to take Veronica in but her only concerns were for the insurance policy money and how much the State would pay her if she took the little fucker in. And because of her selfish ways, Veronica was sent to a foster home to finish living out her nightmares. "Come to think about it she told me she had a little sidepiece down in Houston. Now don't get me to lying. I don't know his name but I heard he was some type of rapper," Ronda said as she took a deep pull on the tightly rolled blunt. She looked at Dre and could tell something was on his mind. "Damn baby, you ain't said two words. Let me give you a backrub to ease your mind." Twenty minutes later Ronda succeeded in accomplishing her mission. "Oh, this dick taste so good (smack, slurp, slurp, smack)." Ronda's head moved up and down to Bryson Tiller's "Don't."

"Damn girl, you doing your thang, shit…you…you…you got the best head a nigga ever (snort, snort) had," Dre said in between every line of powder he snorted off the glass tray.

Ronda's room was laid out and had several X-rated toys lying around. As the Pinky porno DVD played at a low volume, Dre kept his eyes on Ronda's ass that was in the air shaking back and forth. "I got something that's gone really make you feel good," Ronda said as she moved her upper body towards the edge of the bed. After leaning over and pulling a wooden box the size of a small jewelry box from under her bed, she sat on the bed with her legs open. "Just come over here and eat some dessert while I get my zone on," Ronda said while rubbing her fat clit. Dre eyed the box and couldn't believe what Ronda did next. Opening the box, Ronda pulled out a small chunk of what Dre assumed was crack and proceeded to stuff it in a glass pipe.

"Bitch, what the fuck you think this is? You ain't 'bout to smoke that in my face, hoe."

But Ronda was already melting down the crack when Dre jumped off the bed. "Damn baby, just let me blow some on your dick then I'm gone let you fuck me anyway you want; in my ass hole if you want," Ronda said as she took a heavy pull of the pipe and held the smoke in her lungs for what seemed like minutes.

Dre said to himself, "What the hell. Shit can't get no worse anyways," as Ronda exhaled the smoke and took Dre into her mouth. Dre loved every minute of it. "Damn, I wanna hit that shit, too."

Ronda felt good and Dre's comment was right on time. "Oh, you ready to hit this pussy, daddy (slurp, slurp, smack, slurp)?

Dre shook his head, no. "Nawl, I wanna hit that pipe, the big whistle, that glass."

Ronda couldn't believe he was that weak; a real life lame. Her intentions were to fuck and suck him then blackmail him so she could get some of Veronica's money he was sitting on. But now she was about to turn this young street punk out. After teaching Dre how to smoke the pipe, he became a born professional. She let him hit the pipe while she sucked him, fucking his brains out. Another two hours passed and at 4:30 a.m. they were down to crumbs. "Baby, we need to re-up on at least another ounce or two so I can keep that dick hard. Now I got my connect who will hook us up with two zips for twenty-two hundred. You know it's a drought so shit is ugly. But we need to hurry before he goes to sleep," Ronda explained as she rubbed Dre's balls and manipulated his young, dumb mind.

Dre knew what coke was going for, maybe 'bout nine-fifty to eleven hundred a zip and he even had a supplier. But he was far too zooted to let his nigga see him like this. Dre had roughly three stacks in his pocket so it was nothing. After Ronda returned from re-copping they smoked and fucked until the sun came up.

"Daddy, Aunt Ronda, open the door. We hungry," both girls chimed in as they beat their little fists on the bedroom door.

The time on the digital clock read 2:45 p.m. Dre and Ronda had re-upped four times since last night. Dre had spent all his money and spent $5,500 dollars that Veronica had in her checking account. After going to each and every ATM he could find and overdrawing Veronica's account, he was busted, tapped out, zero dollars to his name. "Hold on, girls."

"Damn Dre, move yo' funky ass out my face," Ronda said while rolling her eyes. As Dre lifted up he let out a loud burst of gas.

"Excuse me."

Ronda was still going strong even in the late hours of the afternoon. What she didn't tell Dre was that she was only paying $600 dollars on each transaction then she could tuck away the extra $1,600 dollars on each re-up. After doing that four times she was $6,400 richer. And the truth was that she was only buying half an ounce each time. Dre's dumb-ass was either too high to realize or didn't care.

"Here I come, babies." Ronda took one more pull and her pussy got extra wet. "Dre, did you use all the rubbers already?" she asked with eye pupils the size of quarters.

"Hell yeah, damn, I should have bought another box," Dre whispered as he reached for the pipe and stroked his dick to full erection.

"Fuck that, I got to get some more of that good weenie." Ronda jumped on top of Dre's dick as he lay back, taking a full pull.

"Oh shit! Ronda, you...you..., oh shit, damn, you trippin'."

After a quick three minute fuck, Ronda left the room to shower and tend to the girls. When she returned she got straight to the point. "My boy said he'll give us one last ounce for $700. He said he'll even throw in an extra eight ball!"

Dre was too high to argue, even though he knew he had no money left, he had a plan. "Watch the girls. I'll be back." Dre got dressed and left, thinking about nothing but pussy and crack.

CHAPTER 33

As Paco eyed the snack machine in the break room at the hospital, his pager went off and the PA (Public Address) system requested his immediate assistance in the Intensive Care Unit (ICU). "Dr. Paris to ICU…code red, code red…Dr. Paris to ICU…code red…" As Paco raced to the elevator he was hoping this call wasn't for the young African-American gunshot victim who'd had a roll of bad luck while participating in the Houston All-Star weekend events. Already frustrated that Veronica had stood him up this week, he mashed the button for the 15th floor on the elevator. He had found Veronica on Facebook last month and was in tears as he sat in front of his laptop, looking at her photo along with pictures his granddaughters. After a few attempts at emailing her and requesting a friendship, Veronica finally gave in, but not before letting her father "have it."

The first phone call was hurtful to Paco. She'd said, "Nigga, you left me. Do you know what I went through all those years, do you?" But in reality he did know and he did what any real father would have done. Paco had already lost his sister in a murder/suicide. His niece was dead and his nephew was a livewire in Indiana. Finding his daughter had brought him peace.

* * * * * * * * *

"Sir, like I told you, I can't give out any information on the whereabouts of foster children. If you continue to call and harass me I will turn this matter over to the authorities. Have a nice day, goodbye." Mrs. Pam Johnson hung up on Paco Paris for the third time and final time.

It had been a full two years since the first time he saw or held his baby girl, Veronica. Paco, being the desperate man he had been at the time, decided to go down to Child Protective Services himself and pay Mrs. Johnson a visit. As 5:00 p.m. drew near, Paco waited patiently in the main parking lot. He remembered what Mrs. Johnson looked like from several court appearances so it wouldn't be hard to locate her coming out of the main entrance.

As Pam shut down her computer for the day, she waved goodbye to her co-workers and headed towards the revolving doors which lead to the parking lot. As she walked past McAdoo, the old black security guard, she gave him a fake smile and mumbled "nigger" under her breath. McAdoo smiled, thinking, "I know this cracker is a Trump supporter and don't like me." Pam was truly a racist. As she walked toward her green Honda Accord, Pam felt a bad vibe; the kind you get when you feel as if someone is following or watching you. Pam looked over both shoulders, but after seeing no one, she paid it no mind. Ignoring that intuition would cost her dearly. As she reached for the door handle, she felt a presence behind her back, but before she could turn around it was too late.

"Bitch, don't move, scream or make a scene. Walk straight ahead towards that black Ford Taurus and get in through the driver's door and climb into the passenger's seat.

"Pl...pl...please don't kill me. You can have my purse, my wedding ring, whatever you want. Just don't ki...kill me," Pam mumbled in tears as she followed the strange, but familiar voice giving her instructions.

Once in the Taurus, Paco and Pam exited the parking lot. "I have two words for you, bitch — Veronica Paris." As Paco took the side streets route he had mapped out before the abduction, he spoke out loud and aggressively through gritted teeth about what he wanted from her.

"Oh Lordy, she's living in Acworth, Georgia, about an hour outside of Atl..."

Paco slammed on the brakes and pulled over. "Get to the fucking point! Where's my daughter?" Paco yelled. He didn't intend to hurt this woman, in fact he didn't even have a weapon on him, just an urgency to find the love of his life.

"She's with Sue Brussner. I don't know the address offhand. Please don't hurt me, please! It's in Acworth off of Wade Greene Road. It's a big yellow house next to the Citgo gas station."

Paco got back on the expressway to take Pam back to her jobsite. He reached into her purse and grabbed her I.D. for insurance. "I'm taking you ba…" he started to say but what Pam did next fucked up Paco's stomach. He was driving at the 70 m.p.h. speed limit and he couldn't believe she opened the passenger door and hopped out the car. She literally hopped. "Nooooo! Paco screamed, but it was too late as he watched Pam's tumbling body through his rearview mirror. Then to his horror, her body was hit full speed by an 18-wheeler BP Gas semi-truck. The impact threw her body 55 feet across the expressway into the metal median that separated the north and south expressways. As her body slammed into the metal median her head exploded on impact and her spine was ripped through her back. Her body was wrapped around the metal in such an awkward position that they had to cut the metal into pieces to remove her body later that day. "Dumb bitch!" Paco yelled as he drove to his next location to switch cars. After ditching both stolen cars and setting them on fire with Pam's belongings, he drove off in his car and headed to his baby.

* * * * * * * * *

"Bitch, I told you…I told yo' funky black ass to clean!!" Big Mama, better known as Sue Brussner, yelled as she slapped little Veronica with the handle of the broom. She hit the poor child so hard that the wooden broom handle broke. While on the floor crying and begging for Big Mama to stop, Veronica began to pray, "Please Jesus, I'll be good." This made Sue furious. She felt like she was God. Sue grabbed a skillet full of hot cooking grease and threw the contents in Veronica's direction. The hot, scorching grease spilled all over Veronica's back. "Come on whore. Yeah bitch, I told you!" Big Mama shouted and started dragging Veronica into the bathroom. "Run some water and wash these walls. NOW!" she yelled as she punched the poor child in the mouth. "Matter of fact, scrub the toilet, bitch; take a bath and go to bed!" As Veronica slowly got on her knees, she cleaned the toilet and got in the tub.

Paco had seen enough as he looked through the bathroom window. He quickly ran to the front door and rang the bell (ding-dong). Veronica jumped and so did Sue. "Now who in the hell is this so late?" Sue wondered. She got up and rushed to the door. What happened next, no one ever knew. Veronica was in so much pain she fell asleep in the tub to block it out, only to be awakened later by several police officers. They saw the serious burns on her back when she screamed out as they lifted her out the tub. She had to be airlifted to the children's hospital. The whereabouts of Sue aka Big Mama were unknown. Paco wasn't aware of his daughter's injuries so he gave her a gentle kiss as she lay in the half-empty tub and left the home, but not before making Sue disappear. He knew the authorities would find little Veronica and take care of her. He contacted the police from a burner phone he'd purchased and reported gunshots from Sue's house. Then he got rid of the phone. But after the news of Pam Johnson's death got out, Paco knew Atlanta was too hot for him so he relocated to Houston.

* * * * * * * * *

As Paco exited the elevator, he ran into the surgery theater for patients in critical condition. When he stepped into the cold room which smelled like disinfectant, he almost vomited. "No, God no!!" was all Paco could whisper to himself. He looked down at Slim's body that had tubes running in and out of it.

"Dr. Paris, he's losing a lot of blood and his heart rate is unstable. You're going to have to remove the bullets lodged in his ribcage," the white obese woman said through a blue surgical mask.

"Let me see the x-rays," Paco shouted. He quickly reviewed them as a nurse helped him into his surgical gown. Then he scrubbed up for surgery and went to work on his best friend. Slim was one of the first people Paco met while he was in Houston, running from his past. With not much money to his name, Slim helped Paco through medical school and supplied him with resources he needed to survive in H-town. Whenever one of Slim's homeboys or clients in the NBA got injured, they went to Paco. Anyone in the NFL that Slim dealt with went to Paco.

Paco soon decided to start his own private practice outside of his day job at the hospital. He only catered to elite entertainers and sports players and kept their identities confidential. It didn't matter if they got in an accident on a motorcycle. The league would never know because Paco kept their secrets and would even draw up fake documents stating injuries of some other type, such as a natural slip or fall, or bad knee, etc. to keep the league officials off their backs. Once he found out he was never considered a suspect in the death of Pam Johnson or disappearance of Big Mama, Paco went full throttle. He began to make a ton of money, new friends and he owed it all to Slim.

"I can handle this from here," he told the assisting nurse. He was going to save his friend's life. Suddenly, the operating door flew open.

"Commander, you're not going to believe this. There's another gunshot victim in the room down the hall."

Paco became irritated with the young Mexican doctor. "What does that have to do with the price of crack in Harlem? Can't you see I'm busy saving this man's life?" Paco yelled through his mask. Everyone called Paco "commander" because he ran shit.

"Commander, the woman has your same last name and had this heart-shaped locket around her neck. I do believe you are in this picture with her, sir." The young Mexican doctor extended his hand and opened it, revealing the locket in his palm, showing Paco the picture. It was indeed a picture of a young Paco, Vita and Veronica when she was two-years old.

"Attend to this young man," he told the young Mexican doctor in an urgent voice. "You better treat him as if he's Jesus on his death bed," Paco said as he ran out of the operating theater with tears in his eyes to save his only child. "God, if someone has hurt my little girl I'm going to wake Houston up this All-Star weekend! God, you know I don't bluff!!" he said to himself. He ran down the hall past uniformed officers and burst into the room in tears. "Baby!" The heart monitor began to beep fast and loud.

"Hurry, we're losing her!" The monitor was loud and beeping uncontrollably as it filled the room like a police siren. "Beep-beep-beep-beep-beep-beeeeeeeeeeeepppppp…."

"Apply shock treatment!!" a doctor yelled.

Paco ran over to his baby. Only the young Mexican doctor knew and suspected Veronica might be related to him at this time, otherwise the hospital wouldn't let him treat a relative. This would be the biggest and most important surgery of his life. He owed this to his little angel. "I'm here now, baby," he whispered.

"Clear!"… "Beeeeep!"…"Clear!"… "Beep-Beep-Beep…"

CHAPTER 34

S tuck in deep thought at a red light, Dre pushed himself to stay awake. Firing up another Newport, he was tweaking and fiening for another hit. As he pulled his Honda Civic into a Shell gas station he parked on the side of the building. He reached underneath his seat and found what he was looking for — a .32 revolver that was slightly rusted. "Dear Lord, protect me, forgive me for my sins, but you know what it is." Dre opened his door, inhaling the fresh air. For the first time in a long time he heard birds chirping. He felt relieved. He stuffed the .32 into the waistband of his Sean John jeans and looking normal, he walked into the store. Several people roamed freely around the store. A skinny Asian woman at the instant coffeemaker eyed Dre suspiciously as she made her morning drink.

Walking up to the counter Dre spoke low and clearly, "Listen old man, fill up one of those bags with all the cash, all the scratch-offs and two one thousand dollar Money Orders. And don't make no sudden moves." To show the old man he wasn't bullshitting, he reached into his waistband and pulled out the .32 revolver.

The Asian lady who was set to retire from the Fulton County Sheriff's Office at the end of the year became completely pissed off after seeing Dre pull out a gun. Even though she was carrying an ankle piece which was a .38 snub nose, she had no time for this fuckery. In 25 years she had only fired a gun once at a suspect, and that was a stray dog in a garage.

"Hurry up, nigga," Dre spit as he pointed the firearm.

"Freeze! Don't fucking move! Drop the weapon!"

Boom! Boom! The woman's loud voice caught Dre off guard as he accidentally shot the old man twice in his midsection. Turning around with gun in hand, Dre met his maker. BOOM! BOOM! BOOM! BOOM! BOOM! BOOM! All six shots met their targets. The first shot tore through Dre's pancreas, the second shot his right lung, the third shot into his stomach, the fourth shot was to the collarbone, and the fifth and sixth shots were both to the head.

The Asian officer visited the gun range weekly. She had just been fortunate enough to have never had to shoot a human being in her 25 years on the force; beginner's luck. Dre died instantly. The floor was painted blood red. The other customers who witnessed the shootings were yelling, screaming, cursing or stealing goods. "Fuck, fuck!" the Asian officer yelled as she rushed behind the counter to check on the old man. He was still conscious and clutching a .45 in his hand. "Don't shoot! I'm a cop!" she screamed but it was too late. BOOM! BOOM! The two large slugs ripped through the Asian officer's right eye socket, brushing cigarette cartons with her brains. Both the Asian cop and the old man lay on the floor until they both died and drifted to heaven. Dre wasn't as fortunate. His spirit didn't have to go far at all. He went straight to hell.

CHAPTER 35

A s Paco continued to blow up his nephew's phone, thinking he was probably mad at him and ain't fucking with him since he probably felt he'd turned his back on him; which wasn't the case. Paco was just a busy man. But now he was in an urgent situation and needed the one person he knew would have his back and get the results he needed. As Paco started to hang up, he smiled at the voice he finally heard on the other end.

"Talk."

Paco could tell his nephew was frustrated. Maybe the death of his niece who was his nephew's sister was still bothering him. So Paco broke the ice. "Nut, it's bad. I don't know how to tell you this but…it's…Ver…it's…" Paco broke down into tears and after a few seconds he pulled himself together and spit it out. "It's Veronica…she's been shot."

Nut almost dropped the phone. Instead he dug the pistol deeper into the Captain's temple. As he processed what he just heard, he asked his Uncle Paco, "What's the damage…" but before Paco could answer Nut interrupted him and said, "Never mind, I know what I need to do. Matter of fact, I'm on the next thing smoking." That was actually a throw-off. Nut rarely caught planes or rode buses because he was too hot. Before he hung up, he said something that gave Paco chills. "Unc, this is a life or death question I'm about to ask you so I need an honest answer. What is your father's name?" The phone went silent.

Paco and Nut's mother held a grudge against their father for a very long time. While he was out playing cops and robbers, they would suffer at the hands of their stepmother who hated and despised them. Paco gathered his thoughts, took a deep breath and answered Nut's question. The answer Paco gave confirmed what the old man had told him. Nut had actually kidnapped his own grandfather. But Paco's next words didn't make shit any better.

"Fuck that nigga! Wherever he is he never did shit..." Nut put his phone on speakerphone so the Captain, who was his grandfather, could hear Paco shout "...never did shit for us, the punk-ass Uncle Tom, boot-licking-ass nigga! If he's on his death bed, pull the plug. Fuck him, and that's on my dead sister!"

The old man couldn't believe his ears. He quickly yelled out, "Son...it's me, pops...I'm so...so...sorry. I love you..." But the phone went dead and the room went silent. Both men knew Paco had hung up.

Nut took a deep breath. He knew at some point in his life he had to change. "Well old man, you told the truth. Shit, that's rare for a police officer but I got to turn the ovens on in Texas. It's a lil chilly down there which means this is where we part." BOOM!!!

CHAPTER 36

BOOM!!!

As the doors flew off their hinges several federal agents, including Agent Mondo Taroski, entered Laneka's living room. They were shocked at what they saw in front of them. Captain Smith had been badly beaten, but was alive.

"Where's Sergeant Lewis?" Agent Mondo asked.

"He's...he's...behind..." The Captain was purposely going in and out of consciousness. His grandson had agreed to spare his life and in return Smith would pin everything on Sergeant Lewis; and even make the department and DA believe that Lewis was the mastermind behind everything. "On a lead...lead..." Smith continued to fake symptoms, hoping to buy his grandson time to leave the city and get to Texas. Although Captain Smith was disgusted with Paco's remarks, he still felt guilty about not being there for his son, and especially his daughter, who was Nut's mother.

"The man we are looking for is Sergeant Lewis," Smith barked as agents helped him to his feet. At that very moment Lewis walked through the front door, escorted by two federal agents. "You muthafucka!!" Smith yelled.

Lewis couldn't believe his eyes. He'd expected to find a dead Captain Smith. Lewis quickly reached for one of the agent's firearms and tried to get off a shot at Captain Smith. Unfortunately, he never got that opportunity. Agent Taroski shot Lewis twice in the face, killing him instantly.

To Be Continued...

COMING IN MARCH 2019
CERTIFIED THRILLA PART 3

Also in stores now:

Concrete Walls & Steel Bars: The New Willie Lynch by: Mr. P.D. White (Amazon, Kindle, Barnes and Nobles)

➤ Concrete Wallz & Steel Barz (the album) by: Philthy Phil & StrictlyBiz

➤ (iTunes, Apple Music, Rapbay, CD Baby, Amazon)

➤ Blame it On the Drako (the mixtape) by: Philthy Phil

➤ (Rapbay, Audiobrand, Apple Music, etc)

➤ Back 2 Bizness (the album) by: StrictlyBiz

➤ (Amazon, Apple Music, iTunes)

An Excerpt from...

Certified Thrilla 3

CHAPTER 1

"**T**oday, I didn't even have to use my words to an Ice Cube song as I rental off the exit of the highway,
Uncle Paco's house. He was now in the hot, but beautiful, city
Houston Texas. In his mind it was time to turn the temperature
up just a little more.

"Fuck, nigga, watch where you driving that piece of shit-ass
car!" A dark-skinned teenager with a mouth full of gold
continued to yell and insult Nut as they both waited at a red light.
The boy in the bright lime-green Chevy "Glass House" continued
to stare at Nut, mugging him. "Lame ass nigga, you don't want
no stick play. Let this blower Swiss cheese yo' pussy ass."

As the youngsta accelerated, hitting his gas pedal, Nut just
smiled, shaking his head. He knew it was scorching hot in Indiana
and unless his grandfather was able to make their plans work, he
was going to need a miracle to remain low key. He pulled into a
gas station and noticed the lime-green Chevy pull in right behind
him.

"Yes I'm a rich nigga, rich nigga, rich nigga." Youngboy NBA
blasted from the speakers of the youngsta's Chevy as he pumped
his gas. He continued to mug Nut and felt like Nut was just
another pussy. He'd just gotten his hands on an AK-47 and was
dying to use it. As he sipped his Pepsi he got angry at what he
saw. "Damn, punk ass kids got they lil dirty-ass handprints all on
my pretty-ass candy paint," he said out loud and looked over at
the mini-carwash across the street from the gas station. "Might
as well wipe this bad boy down for I crunch and slam dunk on

...he youngsta was thinking as he finished pumping his

Nut, who was in the gas station store paying for his gas and an almond Snicker bar, kept his eyes on the youngsta. He walked out of the store and noticed the lime-green Chevy was gone. He walked over to his car and his mood instantly changed. There was soda splattered all over the driver's door and window. A Pepsi bottle was lying on the ground as if someone purposely threw it at the vehicle. Nut patiently pumped his gas and grabbed some paper towels from the dispenser above the gas pump. He finished pumping his gas and cleaning up the mess and got into the Nissan, pulling slowly out of the gas station. Paco's house was just around the corner. When Nut was less than 300 feet from the gas station he noticed the lime-green Chevy at the carwash across the street from the gas station. "I need this one," he said to himself.

As Nut pulled up he could hear the loud music coming from the Chevy. He observed the tall, lanky youngsta with his pants sagging, ass out, as he vacuumed the interior of his car. Nut didn't have to sneak up on him because his music was so loud he couldn't have heard an earthquake if one occurred. He stood behind the youngsta for 30 seconds before kicking him in the ass.

"Agh! The fuck!" The youngsta tried to reach over to the passenger seat and grab the AK-47 but Nut beat him to it first.

"Ya'll young niggas talk that stick talk but don't walk that stick walk." BLAHH! BLAHH! BLAHH! BLAHH! BLAHH! BLAHH! BLAHH! The seven quick shots dribbled all over the youngsta's face, chest and even his stomach area. He was killed instantly. Nut was in town and it wouldn't take long for the city of Houston to realize that...

* * * * * * * * *

"Ask me another stupid-ass question. I already told you, ain't no fuckin' restroom stops," the fat, white Correctional Officer (C/O) barked at Drill as he and his partner escorted Drill and several other inmates to the hospital for various reasons. For the past week, Drill and Lucky had communicated on a cellphone Drill had bought on the line in the Houston County Jail. Both had come up with an escape plan. Drill would go to medical for the next week and continue to complain about chest, stomach and lung complications. Drill knew this would cause the doctor to have him taken to an outside hospital for a MRI, biopsy and other evaluations. After the rampage that happened at Doug and Sheila's house, Drill had been charged with triple homicide which consisted of the deaths of Doug, Sheila and one officer. They also charged him with the attempted murder of 10 officers, unlawful possession of firearms and assault rifles as well as the attempted murder of Sheila's daughter, Leslie, who was later found unconscious in her neighbor's backyard. In the state of Texas all of this meant only one thing: DEATH ROW.

Drill called Lucky four minutes after the C/O told him he was going to an outside hospital. "Brah, they 'bout to escort me to the hospital. All we got to do is wait 'til these dumb bitches stop and get some food and then you go to work on them," Drill explained to Lucky.

"Nigga, I got this. These hoe-ass niggas shot Slim so I'm on one, period. Anybody can get it!" Lucky yelled into the phone with courage.

"You dumb muthafucka's ain't getting no damn McDonalds. Y'all got sack lunches 'fo we left the jail, so don't ask. It ain't even a fuckin' option," the fat, white C/O said sarcastically as he got out of the transportation van. "Hey Joe, what you want again? Big Mac meal, three apple pies, supersized fries and supersized diet Coke, righ…" BOOM! BOOM! The two shots from Lucky's

.40 cal. splattered the side of the C/O's face before he got a chance to confirm the order from his partner Joe.

"Wha – what the fuck?" Joe had just witnessed his friend get shot at point-blank range by a madman with a gold tooth. He reached for his holster but his sweaty hands made it difficult to get a grip on his gun. Instead, he pulled out his Taser by mistake. Lucky fired twice, hitting him in his chin and in the center of his neck, killing him instantly. The McDonald's parking lot was erupting into screams, shrieks and cries for help.

"Nigga, hurry the fuck up!" Drill yelled as he and Darryl patiently waited for Lucky to take the keys off the C/O and open the back door of the van.

Just as Lucky opened the back door of the van, Lola pulled up in the getaway car and honked the horn three times. "What you doing? Waiting for backup to arrive? Dumb-ass nigga, hurry up 'fo I pull off!" she yelled.

Lucky paid her no mind. Instead he looked at Darryl. "Drill, move out the way." Lucky aimed his .40 cal. and let off four shots in Darryl's direction.

"Dumb-ass nigga he wit us! This nigga helped distract the driver!" Drill yelled.

"Nigga, he shot my brah, Slim…" Although none of the bullets hit Darryl, they did hit the other two passengers who were both white and arrested for rape and sodomy. As Lucky uncuffed Drill and Darryl he slapped Darryl with the .40 cal. and angrily spit in his face. "I don't wish jail on nann nigga, but after this, I'm gone smoke yo' ass. Fuck what Drill rapping 'bout."

Darryl just smirked and said, "Whatever, son."

CHAPTER 2

The city of Houston had been in a complete state of mayhem during All Star weekend. The police department reported a number of shootings, robberies and multiple homicides. Among the slain was Veronica who succumbed to her injuries sustained in the shootout at the Hotel Derek in Houston. Also, among the dead was the infamous drug lord "Kilo" as well as "Rain" who died in the ambulance on the way to the hospital. Darryl "D-Dub" Washington was arrested when federal agent Tashawn "Taz" Vasquez revealed her identity to the lead detective and requested that he place Darryl under arrest for fear that he would disrupt her ongoing investigation into the drug lord Kilo. Now that Kilo had died from his injuries, Taz realized that had been poor judgment on her part. She had not known just how connected Darryl was and if he'd had any business dealings with RuTristen (aka Tristen), Kilo's son and new target. Since the death of his father, Tristen was developing feelings for Taz in just a week's time.

Taz reached out to Paco and offered her condolences for the death of Veronica. Taz did not reveal to Paco that she was a federal agent but she did tell him that the gunman who killed Veronica was targeting her. She made up a story about Kilo being some weirdo who had been stalking her and Veronica the entire All Star weekend. She even went as far as to lie and say that she held Veronica until the medics arrived and Veronica told her to tell "Daddy I love him." Taz agreed to pay for all the burial expenses.

* * * * * * * * *

"Nephew, I just don't understand. I did all I could as a father." Paco continued to shake his head in anger and frustration as he shed tear after tear while explaining to Nut everything he knew about the situation of Veronica's death. Paco even played several YouTube clips of the shootout to Nut over and over again. Some of the footage was choppy and due to people trying to take cover, whoever was filming the scene with their phone caused the camera to shake and move every time the person filming would duck for cover. One thing about the footage, it was very detailed. Nut was able to see every face of every person involved. He was even able to point out who he believed this Taz character was.

Based on what Paco had told him about Veronica's death and with footage from the chaotic shootout, there was no mistake about who the target had been. In fact, the footage never showed anyone holding or comforting Veronica. It showed a black female using Veronica's body for cover then cowardly running toward the officers. Paco agreed that it didn't make any sense. Why would this Taz person lie? One thing Paco knew about his nephew, he was very professional and thorough about dissecting and breaking every situation down to the facts. So after a few drinks and Nut explaining Keke's death and the situation with his grandfather, he and Paco both agreed that after all of this was over they were definitely leaving the country.

"Unc, now this Slim guy…tell me exactly how you know him and how can he be an asset?"

Paco had received a text from Texas Slim earlier that day letting him know he was out of surgery and alright. When Slim told Paco about Lucky's betrayal, Paco just responded, telling him, "Every dog has his day. You know what you must do now." "Well…I mean shit nephew, Slim basically has his hands in everything down here in Houston. His team of young hitters run the entire 5th Ward, and his son runs the Southside crew. Slim can get you whatever you need: guns, dope, explosives, birth certificates, passports, or whatever." Paco heard a ping and saw he had a text alert. "Shit, this him right here texting me. Hold on…let me call him. He says it's urgent." Paco hit speed dial and called Slim.

Nut just rubbed his palms together in deep thought. He glanced at the AK-47 he took from the youngsta at the carwash and noticed the gold-plated trigger. At least the young nigga had good taste. Looking closer Nut observed the diamond encrusted initials "S.S." on the handle. "These young niggas retar…" but his thought was cut off when Paco raised his hand in the air.

"Hold on, this urgent." Paco was in deep conversation. "What's the link…hold on…carwash…murder…alright. I'ma hit you back Slim." Paco took his phone from his ear and hit the web browser icon and Nut became curious.

"What was that all about, Unc?"

Paco thought his ears were playing tricks on him. "Man, this shit just got real. Some stupid-ass nigga done shot and killed Slim's only son. And Lil Slim's dumb-ass do that damn FaceTime live or Facebook live or whatever that shit is called. The shit is all over the internet; the whole shooting!" Paco pulled up the link and played the clip as he and Nut watched. "Shit, his music so damn loud you can't hear shit…wait…hold on. I think this is where he gets shot." Due to the position of the phone, the only thing the video clip captured was the barrel of the AK-47 and the footage did not reveal who the shooter was. Nut and Paco just shook their heads and said, "That's fucked up."

CHAPTER 3

Darryl knew that his current situation was no better than his previous one in a jail cell. Due to multiple surgeries on his knees in the past, he had to see a specialist on a regular basis in order to get medication for nerve damage, pain and blood thinners. When Drill got into the van that day to be transported to the hospital, he and Darryl hit it off. They'd both seen each other's case on the news so they had a mutual respect as soon as they met. Darryl was completely in the blind about the escape plan. His only intention was to bribe the driver to get him and the others a few items from McDonalds. His distraction of the officer allowed Lucky to execute his plans without bringing attention to himself. Drill liked his cockiness so he pleaded with Lucky not to shoot him.

Back when he was arrested, Darryl continued to run the entire week through his mind, over and over again. How did Rain end up dead? How did Kilo end up dead? How did Veronica end up dead? And who was Taz? Darryl recalled seeing her run towards the police and shortly thereafter they chased him through the emergency exit and cornered him outside. Darryl knew that no one knew he was involved other than his boy Rain, Kilo, Veronica and Taz. He also knew that no one saw him sneak towards the emergency exit but Taz. And from the back of the squad car he could have sworn he saw Taz and his new buyer, Sosa, both talking to the feds. He also vaguely remembered seeing Sosa get into the back of an ambulance and never exiting it. At that time Darryl's mind was in a state of trauma.

"Nigga, let it be known we ain't on the same team, hoe-ass nigga," Lucky yelled, snapping Darryl out of his trance.

Darryl knew that Rain was responsible for the shooting and possible death of the guy he'd seen Lucky with. Now, after hearing Lucky talk, he guessed it was his brother. After the detectives finished charging Darryl for all his crimes, his police report failed to mention Rain's name at all so Darryl blamed Rain for everything. "Son, you wiling out. That bitch-ass nigga I was wit aired yo' peoples out yo'." Lucky turned around in the passenger seat and pointed his gun at Darryl.

Lola screamed, "You two feminine-ass niggas need to calm down while I'm driving. And Lucky, you need to tell me where I'm fucking driving!" She couldn't believe she put herself in the middle of a prison escape and a double homicide. In her mind, Lucky was a fuckin' showoff and didn't have to kill the C/O's. Now her scandalous ways had her deeper than she was willing to go.

"She right, brah! Aye baby, keep driving until you pull up to this next right and then take a left." Drill calmed the situation down as he gave Lola directions. He liked this little yella "jazzy" thing. Shit, in his mind, he was ready to fuck. "Lucky, next time you point that pistol near me and don't squeeze, we gone have issues. We got bigger problems and you acting like you this hitter all of a sudden… Stay in yo' lane, matter of fact, baby girl, pull over to the side of the highway. Lucky, you fent to get yo' ass in the back and I'm sitting in the front." Drill checked Lucky like the lame he was. All Darryl could do was laugh.

"Finally, a fuckin' boss nigga," Lola said. As she was about to pull over she changed her mind and kept going. "Nawl, fuck both of y'all. Nigga, you got on fuckin' jail clothes and we on a busy street. Only reason we ain't hot cause we riding tints. If anything, we not stopping til we get to wherever it is we going."

Drill didn't like her attitude and the fact that she questioned his authority. "Brah, pass me that stick real quick," Drill barked at Lucky.

A little pissed off at Drill's earlier remarks, Lucky thought about shooting his tough ass. But he was in such fear of Drill he thought the gun might jam up. Without a word, Lucky reached back and handed the gun to Drill.

Drill then handed the pistol to Darryl. "Aye D, let me see how you push a line."

Darryl lit up like a Christmas tree and said, "I thought you'd never ask." As Darryl mugged Lucky he pushed the barrel of the pistol into the back of Lola's head. "Bitch, you done witnessed some real live gangsta shit! I ain't into smoking bitches but I ain't into going back to jail, so that lil attitude 'bout to shift from 60 to zero or you can get your wings right now." Darryl was pissed off at how Lucky handled him and he never liked Lola anyway. Right now he could kill the entire car. Then he got a sick, sinister idea. "Matter of fact, I'm not feeling none of this. As of now I'm running the show."

Everyone went silent and for the next fifteen minutes they drove in complete silence. For Drill, this was no issue. He knew if he took command both Lola and Lucky would be dead. Drill never even considered Darryl's words as a threat or even a factor in his current situation.

Lola told herself if she lived to see the end of this, all three of these niggas would suffer.

CHAPTER 4

"Oh my fuckin' god… Get this good pussy daddy! Yes, yes, yes! Tristen, oh…I'm… 'bout…cum…FUCK!!'" Taz shouted as she rode Tristen's dick. She came and climaxed in pure ecstasy. Although she had an ulterior motive for fuckin' with Tristen, Taz could not deny the fact that she was also having strong feelings for Tristen.

As Taz got out of the bed to use the bathroom, Tristen looked at her round, plump ass and admired it until she shut the bathroom door. "Girl, hurry up so daddy can get it in again," Tristen yelled as he heard the shower start in the luxurious hotel room. Looking around the room all Tristen could envision was his father. He was now out here in this world alone. For some strange, sick reason he felt as if he knew Taz. "This bitch ain't been in my D.M. and I don't recall her at no strip joints," he said to himself. He grabbed his phone to check his Instagram account and upload photos of his father. But when he went to use his phone it was dead. "Fuck!" he swore.

He saw Taz's phone on the night stand on the other side of the bed. "Shit, I hope this bitch ain't tripping," he thought as he tried to gain access into her phone. Her "enter passcode" screen kept popping up. Due to his street connections on burner and stolen phones used for business dealings, Tristen knew several reset codes for different model phones from Boost, Metro PCS, Sprint, Apple, AT&T, etc. After typing in an administrative reset code, Tristen was able to gain access into Taz's phone. He was betting on this lil thot having some hella-ass pictures of herself in there and his plan was to forward them to his phone. However, as he scrolled through Taz's photos he saw pictures which made his stomach turn.

"What the fuck you doing, nosey-ass nigga?" Taz called out as she sprinted across the room like a gazelle. By the time she reached her phone the "enter passcode" screensaver had popped up which didn't reveal Tristen had gained access.

"Damn shawty, my phone is dead. I couldn't even get in yo' shit wit all yo' lil security shit..." Tristen was in his finesse mode. He knew he'd seen Taz somewhere and he now had a plan for her little slick ass. "Let's go out to eat today," Tristen said.

Taz ignored him as she went through her phone. As soon as she entered her passcode her screen returned to her photo gallery and the screen image showed her nemesis, Kilo. Although Tristen thought he was slick, Taz knew she was slicker and decided to play this little game of his. She knew she'd seen his father's photo. Now Taz had to protect herself and the integrity of the FBI. Tristen would have to go.

* * * * * * * * *

The room stood in complete silence as Texas Slim spoke. "Any nigga you hear about trying to sell my son's choppa, you bring that nigga to me. Period. Everybody know Lil Slim the only nigga who had a AK-47 modified, customized and engraved with diamonds which read 'S.S.' for 'Southside'. So, if the nigga or niggas sell it, more than likely they gone dump it in Dallas, Port Arthur, San Antonio or out of state. To sell it in Houston would be suicide. But then again, that's all these young niggas commit nowadays. Y'all know it's a gold-plated trigger on it also. So keep your eyes and ears open."

While Slim spoke, not one person interrupted. The room was cluttered and reeked of loud cush smoke. The house was located on the Southside in one of the hoods where Lil Slim moved large quantities of weed. Texas Slim never allowed his son to move cocaine, although he'd heard stories that his son had begun to do so. It was also no secret that his brother, Lucky hated his nephew. He felt like Texas Slim would bless his son with large quantities of product but wouldn't give him anything compared to what Lil Slim got. On a few separate occasions Texas Slim had to check Lucky and tell him, "Brah, you a grown-ass man, you not my son. All that Lil Slick side busta shit ain't gone fly!" When Texas Slim spoke no one who knew him dared to interrupt, not even his brother.

"The first one of you niggas who bring that choppa to me and the nigga who sold it to you, I got 20 bands and my SS Chevelle on 8ˢ for you." The entire room burst into jeers and even a few whistles.

"Aye Slim, if I catch the nigga who smoked brah, I'm gone kill 'em myself, fuck that!" Young Paper was a new booty fresh off his grandma's porch. Everybody told him he talked too much. In Young Paper's mind if he could impress Texas Slim, he'd be next up to run Southside.

"Is that right…?" Texas Slim shifted his attention to the young, dirty kid who spoke such nonsense. "And what makes you think you can break my instructions playah…what's yo' name?"

As Slim reached inside his black hoodie, Young Paper smiled and happily gave Slim his name. "They call me Young Paper and I been telling these niggas me and you need to meet. I'm telling you Slim, I GO. All my 40ˢ got 30ˢ on 'em and I be smashing. One nigga I was into it wit back home in Utah, I had to whip out on 'em…" BOOM! BOOM! BOOM! BOOM! BOOM! BOOM!

BOOM! All seven shots from Slim's .44 Desert Eagle hit Young Paper above the waist; and into his chest and face.

"Anybody else got some plans?" Texas had spoken. Everybody was prey.

"Brah, what you do that for? You just shot my fuckin' brother!" The short, fat boy the hood called Pie Face rushed to his brother's aid.

"Damn, this nigga was yo' brother?" Texas Slim asked as he kicked the dead body of Young Paper.

Everyone else in the room remained silent. This group of young men was Lil Slim's soldiers. Some of them were gangstas but the rest were strays, leeches, dope fiends and suspect. Texas had warned his son that these dudes weren't built like they claimed to be. Young Paper and Pie Face were originally from Salt Lake City, Utah. Pie Face had a quick temper and was known to get off first. Young Paper had a hustle-hand but his lust for mollies, coke and Zaney bars had him zoned out.

"Hoe-ass nigga, you gone kill 'em then kick 'em? Youse a bi…" BOOM! BOOM! The two shots into the back of Pie Face's skull opened his head up like a drop-top '72 Impala.

"Oh…that was sexy. Nephew, yo' lil murda game a lil saucey," Slim said.

Texas Slim's nephew, Bad Luck, shoved his .380 back into the waistband of his black 501 Levi's after he shot Pie Face. Bad Luck was Lucky's 13-year old son. He was ruthless, untamed and a hyena. "I didn't like him anyways, Unc. They both talked too much."

Texas Slim threw up the deuces and left the spot. Everyone in the house knew what to do with the bodies.

Made in the USA
Lexington, KY
03 May 2019